ONLY YOU CAN LOVE ME

TRINITY LAKES ROMANCE BOOK FIFTEEN

CAROLYN MILLER

PROLOGUE

WANTED:
Someone hardworking, honest, humble, with a sense of humor, who can appreciate the simple things in life. Who loves God, loves family, and loves animals. Genuine seekers only.

CHAPTER ONE

Valentine's Day. Was any day on the calendar tougher for a single newly crowned twenty-eight-year-old gal than February fourteen? Call her weird but she'd never liked this day. Pink hearts and chocolates and romance everywhere? Please.

But actually… please?

Jessica Martin—Doc Martin to locals—blinked at herself and blew out a breath, taking care not to inhale too deeply. Working as a vet certainly had its joys, but drinking in the aromas of bull and cow dust was not one of them. She reached deeper, her plastic-encased arm stuck two thirds of the way in a cow's behind, her gloved hand desperate to grasp the tiny hooves of the calf, as the seconds slipped away.

"Feel anything?" Jackson Reilly asked.

She slid him a look. His brow was furrowed, as well it should be. This birthing was the latest from his prize bull Brutus, and offspring like this was essential to keep the Reilly ranch progressing. But this was the poor cow's first birth, and she'd been at it so long she was tiring. As was Jess.

She stretched a little deeper. *Please Lord*. Then, "I touched it!"

"Thank goodness." He pushed up his cowboy hat and wiped his brow. "Whew. You had us going there for a moment."

Her fingers gripped the slippery hoof—hard to do when her own hand was sheathed in plastic—and she tugged.

Jackson's own hand was too big, otherwise he'd never have called her. Even Ellie Reilly—soon to be Cohen—was too large. But while Jess's frame might be considered petite by some, she'd always been strong and wiry with a grip that had taken many an older man by surprise when they shook hands. She gritted her teeth, braced her feet, and with her other hand on the cow's rump, carefully maneuvered the calf into position. "Come on, girl."

With a grunt and a moan, which earned a bellow of concern from Brutus, stationed nearby in the Reilly's old red barn, the cow shifted position, then hunkered into position as she slowly pushed out the calf. Jess swiftly withdrew her arm, careful to avoid the contractions which could crush a careless appendage, and watched as the calf slowly made its appearance. Tiny feet first, spindly legs, then the white vernix-covered body.

The cow turned, licking the coat off the calf's face, the rough tongue forcing the calf to take its first breath.

Jess smiled. Some might call what she did disgusting but this was what being a veterinarian was all about. New life. Preserving life. Helping creatures in trouble find a way to live. She *loved* her job. Even if—she rubbed her aching arm, ripping off the plastic arm guard and gloves before stretching out her too-tight hands—it sometimes felt like her job didn't love her. She rolled her neck from side to side, the pop and crackle of tired tendons and facet joints drawing a smile from Ellie.

"You need a coffee, right?"

More than one. After this she had a list of jobs to attend to the length of both her legs. Why all of the animals of Trinity Lakes and surrounds had decided to wait to have their issues until Jess's parents had left on their latest cruise she didn't know. Her lips twisted. Maybe the animals just preferred her methods to those of her father, even if their owners for the most part would prefer Dr. James Martin. But when her dad's ill-health a couple of years ago had forced him to take a back seat in the family veterinary business, she'd had to step up, which meant taking on his workload as well as her own.

While her dad still helped out occasionally, there wasn't a lot he could do while sailing the Caribbean. Apparently that first trip two years ago had given her parents a taste for buffets and sunshine and relaxing, the likes of which they'd never had the chance to do while here in Trinity Lakes. Besides, she didn't want to be going to ask her dad every time something felt hard. How was anyone ever going to learn to trust her if she couldn't trust herself? As it was, she was fairly sure Jackson, or at least some of his siblings, had wondered about her expertise. It hadn't passed her notice that the ranch manager Denny Graham still seemed to think she was the same kid who'd often visited the Reilly ranch when she was younger, as one of Cooper Reilly's classmates. Her stomach soured.

"A coffee would be great, but you might need to make it to go." She offered an apologetic smile. "I'm pretty sure all that beeping on my phone before was Mrs. Cohen about their new puppy, so I'll need to scram."

"You're always so busy," Ellie said, as she helped Jess collect her things.

"That's me. No rest for the wicked."

"Or the best vet in the county," Jackson said. "Thanks for all your help today."

She nodded. "You know you've always got it." She made a kissy face at Brutus, who sniffed and turned away. Just like his owner's brother.

Ugh. She was *not* thinking on him again.

She snatched up her equipment, shrugging into her fleece-lined jacket then tugged the wool beanie over her ears. The recent weather was hardly conducive to sauntering outside in short sleeves. Layering up in merino thermals and lined-jeans was the only way to go when it was still minus temperatures outside.

The Reilly's dog, Fido—yes, that was seriously the poor creature's name—sniffed at her heels, and she rubbed her head automatically.

"Have you heard from Cooper lately?" Ellie asked, as they moved from the barn across the snow-shrouded yard back to the house.

Her heart squeezed. So much for not thinking on him. "Nope."

"Huh. We haven't heard from him lately either."

Jess's breath frosted the air as she released a silent huff. That was no surprise. Cooper Reilly only ever did what Cooper Reilly wanted to do, then expected everyone to fall in line. She was living proof of what happened when they didn't.

"I didn't mean to pry." Ellie's voice held an apology. "I just never understood what went wrong between you two."

Jess shrugged. Truth be told, neither had she. But endless hours of speculation had not helped any, so as a New Year's resolution she'd given up thinking about him. And while the resolution might've worked as well as her efforts to do cardio each day and avoid chocolate, at least she'd come to a certain place of acceptance. Cooper Reilly was just as much of a workaholic as she, and any thoughts of a possible future were pointless when he lived in California and had made it clear he saw no future in Trinity Lakes, Washington. They'd argued, in front of the whole town it seemed, at last year's opening of the Trinity Lakes Historical Museum. One of the more epically embarrassing moments of her life. And considering she'd once had a donkey fart in her face during the Trinity Lakes Christmas pageant, thus ensuring her role as Mary would never be forgotten, her argument with Cooper Reilly had been as savage and humiliating as it was public. Slicing their friendship in two.

Ellie slid open the cozy farmhouse's glass back door, and Jess reveled in the welcome warmth. "Feel free to use the bathroom."

"Thanks." Jess walked to the peach 80s-inspired bathroom, glad for the excuse to escape Ellie's unsubtle interrogation. Why was she still bothered about this after all these months? Good thing she'd soon have someone else to think about.

The smell of coffee drifted to her, summoning her to the kitchen. A glance at the big farmhouse clock drew a wince. "I really should get going."

"Not before you drink this." Ellie passed over a tall to-go cup with Cohen's Hardware emblazoned on the outside.

"Thanks." She took a sip. "That's really good."

"I know." Ellie's smug smile faded as her brow wrinkled. "Are you okay? You look tired."

Awesome.

"Oh, I didn't mean it like that. I'm just worried about you."

Her friend's concern drew an unwelcome burn at the back of her eyes. She blinked hard—how tired was she?—and forced a smile. "Thanks, it's okay. I am tired, and you know I've never been too good at hiding how I feel."

"One of the things I like about you."

Yep, she'd never possessed the luxury of masking her thoughts. She'd always had one of those faces that people could read a mile away. Nobody need ever guess what she was think-ing. Except—her heart skipped—she bet nobody would ever guess one thing about her. What would any of her friends say if they knew she'd signed up for Dream Match?

She took another sip, the warmth begging her to linger. The long list of appointments would still be there regardless of whether she left this instant or stayed a minute or two. Ellie's mom came in, and the two Reillys chatted about an upcoming booking for the Reilly Ranch's farm stay before veering to Ellie's plans for a special Valentine's Day dinner with Jasper Cohen. The bright gleam of Ellie's diamond-clad finger drew a fresh reminder of why Jess had signed up for the new dating app.

The new app was different to so many others in that it required the woman to make the first move with any potential matches, so there were less creepy dudes reaching out, which made it less icky than some apps she'd researched. The app also didn't include photos, so instead of being a shallow pool of random hook-ups it meant people had to dig a little deeper and actually get to know the other person.

And while there were still a lot of loose gooses out there—someone with a handle called TrippyWildMushroom had been an instant swipe left—there seemed to be a fair amount of people genuinely looking for love. She'd only joined yesterday, but already she'd been matched with eight guys within her 'dream match range,' which felt almost miraculous. Why hadn't she ever encountered these guys in real life?

She still felt embarrassed about having to use a dating app to find a date, but the fact she didn't have to post a photo, and could choose a pseudonym, gave her a feeling of security and safety. She'd been surprised at how many professionals there were in rural areas looking for love. Given Trinity Lakes' recent success with romance she didn't think there were any eligible singles of appropriate age and interest left. And anyway, if by some random chance someone around here had gotten onto the brand-new website, how many people around here would guess that BlessBess was Trinity Lakes' local vet?

She thanked Ellie for the coffee and made her way to the red Dodge with Martin's Veterinary Services stenciled on the outside. A big practical truck for little-yet-practical her.

Slamming the door closed—Big Red didn't do gentle suggestions so force was always necessary—she pulled out her phone, stealing another moment of stillness before the next job took her energy. A quick tap and the app opened, and she sipped her coffee, as a prayer rose. *Lord, I know I'm not everyone's cup of tea, but if You've got someone for me, help me find him, and help him find me.*

She sucked in a deep breath and began reading through the profiles that Dream Match thought as potential contenders. Still, just reading profiles didn't mean anything would change. If she wanted to change then she needed to do something different. Like swiping right on a profile she liked, then hoping he'd like what he saw—or didn't see—and swiped right too. A glance at the dashboard clock said she'd have to go soon, but a moment more...

She blinked. Truly? She read the profile again, at the qualities he'd listed as important: humor, faith, family values, hard work. BizC—she smiled at the pun—seemed like a match made in heaven. Her pulse increased, her finger trembled, and with another prayer, she couraged up and swiped right. Then shakily exhaled.

It was now up to him to swipe right and let her know if she matched what he was looking for. And if he didn't, then after twenty-four hours the match would dissolve, and it was clearly not meant to be.

But that was okay. God could use anything to bring Mr. Right across her path. Even a dating app. And so she'd leave it to Him to turn the heart of the right man at the right time toward her, even if she was helping matters along by making herself more available to be found.

Surely someone in this world would want to get to know someone like her. Even if the someone she'd once thought might hold her future had made it very clear she did not hold his.

———

COOPER REILLY SCROLLED through his phone as he ate his sandwich. Some might call him arrogant and entitled but they weren't the ones seeing him sitting at his cubicle during his lunch break eating a homemade sandwich of chicken and salad on rye. He was fairly sure that Jackson and Ellie thought he took three-hour five-star steak lunch breaks on those days when he wasn't playing at the corporate in-office miniature golf course, one of the perks for working for Manson IQ.

The tech start-up had always prided itself on offering perks they hoped rivaled those found at Google's headquarters, such as free food, nap pods, and free employee laundry services, as well as a dedicated "games zone" with table tennis, a pool, and miniature golf. And while he knew some of his colleagues took advantage of those activities, he'd always seen himself as being a little more principled, making sure he did the work they paid him so well for. Yeah, he might be on par with his NHL brother's ridiculously high pay checks, but he worked hard for it. And while people might applaud Mitchell's muscles and on-ice skills they didn't always seem to appreciate Cooper's brain, or want to recognize that as being worthy of appropriate reward.

As the smartest brother of the Reilly clan, Cooper had studied his way to the top of his class, which had taken him to MIT and seen him head-hunted by Apple, before he'd joined Manson IQ two years ago. And he loved it here, even if there were rumors swirling concerning cutbacks. That was par for the course these days. Tech companies were like so many other major corporations, always looking at their bottom line. Heck, even England's royal family was into downsizing and "slimming down" their operations. But Manson IQ would never touch him. His role was too important. Besides, his contract was locked up tighter than Fort Knox.

He shoved the last of his sandwich in his mouth, leaving the crusts. If he was at home on the ranch he'd give the crusts to Fido, but here he'd shove it in the food scrap compost bin that got taken by one of the local green-waste companies and turned into energy. The proliferation of such companies in recent years might be because they thought all the tech stuff centered here in Silicon Valley needed offsetting by environmentalists with a clue. Whatever. He did his bit, or tried to, even if he'd never be as green as the Reilly ranch neighbors Liam and Elissa Darcy might like.

His phone dinged with a notification. He tapped the screen, his eyes widening a little. Someone had hearted his profile?

He read through his message again. Was it the "genuine seeker" that had snagged the interest of someone like that? Maybe it was the mention of God. Or the requirement of "must love animals." To be truly honest, he wasn't super crazy about animals but he figured it had to show a sense of care and connection that backed up any claim about being genuine. The most genuine person he'd ever known had been crazy about animals, so he figured this was a good litmus test of any future girlfriend. He tapped on the profile, lips twitching as he read a profile that was almost word-for-word the same as his. Huh. Seemed these algorithms hadn't had to work too hard to find a contender for a match there. He read through it, then with a prayer, swiped right.

Boom! They had a dream match, which was animated onscreen with a puff of pink smoke he guessed was supposed to look cute but kinda looked cheesy, and so not his scene. Except going on a dating app to find love had never been part of his scene or part of his plan either. He'd had a plan but she hadn't played along, which meant resorting to something like this where the focus was on who he was rather than what he looked like or how much money he made.

He peered at her profile picture, now that the Dream Match had unblurred it, then smiled. It was a photo, taken at a distance from behind, one hand on a straw cowboy hat as the brunette stared at a sunset-washed lake. A picture, just like his, that hinted of features but gave little away, which was the bare minimum requirement to verify an account as genuine, which demanded photos of participants along with LinkedIn profiles (kept private) to ensure genuine applicants who were actually people and not just bots.

His heartbeat increased. Now the ball was in her court. She had twenty-four hours to send him a message, otherwise their dream match would expire. But as she was the first to pique his interest, he really hoped she'd start messaging soon.

"Yo, Coop," Tyson Cleary, his line manager, called. "Trav and Trace want you."

He mentally blinked and refocused. Work, that's right. He shoved his phone in his pocket and nodded to Tyson, then collected his lunch scraps. He disposed of them in the receptacle marked "food waste" then moved down the hall for his interview with Travis Smith and Traci Jolep, the two executives he reported to. His was a weird role, where he was technically under Tyson's supervision, but often used for special projects by T and T, as the staff called them. And given they'd started Manson IQ, they probably deserved the pun as they were a dynamite partnership. He stopped by the bathroom, checked himself in the mirror. Travis might be cool with mini golf in the office but Traci was a stickler for professional attire, and sandwich crumbs on shirts was a no-go in her book.

A minute later he was being invited by Travis to take a seat in the executive office.

He gauged their expressions, but their poker faces were far better than his. Why he was here was a mystery. Was it the crypto app? He'd had his doubts, but it was going better than he'd expected. Or maybe the Trawnly Project had hit a snag. He hoped not, because the hours spent on that project had likely been the cause of his first gray hair, which he was far too young for. But no. It couldn't be that, surely. He found a smile. "Good to see you both."

Two head nods met him, their smiles small, but they hadn't got to near the top of their game by spending time being gushily friendly. Well, Travis could put it on sometimes, but Traci was what old Mrs. Darcy from next door might call a cold fish.

"Thanks for coming in," Travis said.

"Of course." Like he had a choice.

"Cooper, you know we pride ourselves on being upfront, so I'm afraid that there's no easy way to say this."

Cooper's smile dissolved as Travis looked at Traci, who sighed and took the lead.

"We're restructuring, and your role at Manson IQ has been a casualty of that restructure."

He blinked. "I beg your pardon?" She hadn't just said what he thought, had she?

"I'm real sorry, Coop," Travis said. He was always the more conciliatory one. "But as you know many companies like ours have been experiencing some tough times of late, and we've needed to downsize, which means we're unfortunately going to have to say goodbye to some of our most valuable assets."

"What?"

"You're being let go, Cooper," Traci said slowly, as if he was an idiot.

Heat rose in his chest, burning the filter from his words. "I understand that, thanks, Traci. What I don't understand is why. Why me? How can you say I'm one of your most valuable assets and then fire me in the next breath?"

"To be fair *I* didn't actually say you were one of our most valuable assets," Traci said, not blinking.

Right now he wished for a single Southern gene that would enable him to bless her heart with all the sarcasm he could find. But that was Traci for you. Black and white to a fault. Gray was not in her vocabulary.

Travis winced, shooting Cooper a look as if he was person-ally pained by this conversation. If Traci was all head, then

Travis was all heart, wearing emotions on his sleeve like someone else Cooper had known. But that passion was what had gotten things done, and Travis had a passion that had ignited enthusiasm from so many others. Including Cooper.

"We're really sorry." Travis said that in such a genuine-sounding way that Cooper was almost inclined to believe him. "I know this is unexpected. It's been a horrible day, having to tell so many people their roles are finishing up."

So, this really was real? He cleared his throat, shooting for some of Traci's directness. "I'm sorry, but I still don't understand why you are getting rid of me."

"Your salary," Traci said, with another of those long, cool, non-blinking looks. "We can't afford you anymore."

"Why not? My work here has brought in millions of dollars of extra revenue, and—"

"I'm afraid the deal is done." Travis put on his sad puppy-dog eyes.

The man was good at making people feel like he cared. Stupid Coop for falling for it. "What deal?"

"We are consolidating resources with another company, Charles, Henderson and Ipika—"

His lips flattened. He knew CHI. Everyone knew. They were all about energy technology, a global presence with offices both here in North America and in Asia.

"—and we'll be rebranding in the near future."

"As what? Charles Manson?"

Traci stared. "It's not confirmed, but that is an option."

One he now *really* hoped they'd take. Were they kidding? Who'd want to deal with a company named after a notorious killer? Except Traci never joked. The humorous bone had never entered her body. He folded his arms. "So how long have I got?"

"We've got one month before we're announcing this publicly. The boards of both companies have been in negotiations for months, and—"

And nobody had picked up on the cult killer connection? This was insane.

"—will be able to recompense you accordingly, if you choose to resign today."

Wait—what had he just missed? He tracked back through the conversation. "You're saying either I offer my resignation now and score a fat pay check in severance, or I don't stay, but either way access to my work has been revoked?"

"That's right. But if you sign today you'd still be recompensed appropriately," Travis said.

"But not nearly as appropriately as someone who actually is one of your most valuable assets, right?" He blew out a breath. "Excuse me for feeling shocked." Mighty ticked would work, too.

"If you'd prefer to be fired, and not gain access to your severance pay, that can be arranged," Traci said.

Man, she was cold. She could teach the Wicked Witch of the West a few tricks. Mitchell could probably learn a few icy moves from her too. Cooper's gaze narrowed. "I think I'd like to talk to HR, and see exactly what I'm entitled to, thanks."

"Dude," Travis again, as though he thought himself a surfer like Tyson, "like I said, I'm real sorry." He pushed a piece of paper across the desk. "Have a read, see if the amount circled there seems fair—we talked to our lawyers and pay admin and they said it's more than fair—and sign it and we'll get the ball rolling. Otherwise, you'll have to take your chances when CHI and Manson combine."

Combine to become Manson Chi? Nobody needed that kind of negativity in their life. And he certainly didn't need to hang around begging for a job from people who clearly wanted him gone. He snatched up the paper, glanced at the circled figure, and nearly choked. Okay, well, that number certainly would help to sweeten the deal. Half a mill to immediately leave, in addition to his accrued unused leave? And a generous benefits scheme for a year? And—he checked the clauses—no waiting time to find a new job?

He glanced at T and T, who'd just blown up his world. "Fine." He scrawled his name.

"Like I said," Travis said, "I'm really—"

"Sorry, yeah, I heard you the first time." A glance at Traci revealed she was as stone-faced as ever.

He jerked his chin, and pushed to his feet, escaping the office before his shock spewed out in more non-gracious behavior. Whoa. He turned the corner, placed a hand on the wall for balance. He had zero desire to return to the office and face people and try to explain. He needed out. Now.

"Dude?"

Tyson. Great.

"Oh, don't tell me they're getting rid of you too."

Too? "Did you get your marching orders as well?"

"Nope, they're keeping me on." Tyson's sympathetic face couldn't quite hide his relieved glee, which only exacerbated Cooper's frustration.

Seriously? They were keeping Tyson on but getting rid of Cooper? Good luck to them, then. They'd really need it.

"Gotta go," he muttered, shouldering past Tyson in a boss move he reckoned Mitchell would be proud of. Yeah, he might be proving to be a bit of a jerk right now, but how many times had he needed to clean up Tyson's mess? Well, T and T would soon see their mistake. Maybe that was part of the problem, he thought, steaming back to his desk, shutting down his computer, snatching up his personal items, as his mind played with a hundred different scenarios. If his name started with T, then maybe he'd be one of the chosen ones, too.

His hands clenched. Now he really was being stupid. But whatever. He was out of here. His overtime these past two years meant he'd qualified for a ridiculous amount of leave, which he was going to take, starting right now with sick leave.

Because he was sick of working for people who clearly didn't want him, sick of propping up their business, and sick of pretending this was what he wanted in life.

Happy Valentine's Day? Yeah, right. The only happy thing about today was Dream Match girl, and even then it wasn't guaranteed that she'd send him a message within the twenty-four-hour window. Was this even worth doing?

It seemed like it was way past time to take stock and reconsider a whole bunch of things. And the best place to do that? Back home, where life had a way of sifting through the dross and finding what was really real. Back home, at the Reilly ranch. Back home in Trinity Lakes.

CHAPTER TWO

Jess yawned as she slowly drove down Trinity Lakes main street. Past the historical museum. Her stomach tensed and she quickly shifted her gaze away. There was the vintage cinema. Organics store. All decorated in hearts and romance. Last month's massive snowstorm had seen a reduction in town visitor numbers, and Valentine's Day, the first major celebration of the year, was something many local businesses were using by way of offering special dinner packages in an attempt to draw in customers and escape the cold and ice.

Dark tire tracks marked the snowy road which was over-laden with geometric patches where the quaint town lamps and windows spilled golden light from hope-filled restaurants, like the Bellbird Café and Joe's Diner. Ellie and Jasper Cohen were probably there, or at the Country Club, or Giovanni's, the Italian restaurant renovated by Jake Monroe last year. Maybe one day she too would know what it was like to celebrate a special day with someone special.

She rubbed bleary eyes, her fingers itching to check her phone. She'd needed to charge it again after running down the battery at the second last job, and already about a million notifications were awaiting attention tonight. She wondered if her dream match had thought to swipe right on her.

And if he did…

Her mouth dried. What would she say? Two swipe rights meant she'd have to open the conversation, and she had no clue what to say. She probably should've thought this through a little more—a lot more—but she'd been so busy juggling work commitments and running the veterinary practice's admin that she could barely keep up. And if she was so busy that she couldn't even figure out how to open a conversation, then how on earth would she ever manage to squeeze in a real date? Maybe this was a bad idea. She probably should've just put this on the backburner for a while, at least until Mom and Dad returned and Mom could help run the veterinary practice's administration again. Maybe then she'd catch her breath. Juggling administrivia and the actual work of caring for animals was exhausting.

She stifled a yawn and turned into Wainscott Drive, then took a right into her street, the street where she'd lived with her parents all her life, apart from the years she'd spent at university. Living with her parents might sound lame, except it made for a super short commute to work, given the clinic was in the converted garage of the family home.

She turned into her drive, drove past the clinic and remoted open the garage door that had kept Big Red snug and snow free in recent days. Two minutes later she was saying hello to the four cats that had taken up residence in recent weeks. Mom's soft heart was always finding room for strays, and for some reason she liked to name the cats after English queens. So there was Anne, Mary, Vicky and Bess. Bess was the newest, and a friendly, prowly kind of cat, ginger-haired like the original Elizabethan queen, and the opposite of the black-and-white haughty cat that Mom had named after Queen Victoria. God bless Bess for her vibrant nature, for the way she often sought attention and drew Jess from staying too long in her own head. Bess was far more of a social creature than Jess had ever been, so choosing her name was both a sign of gratitude and reflected Jess's aspiration to be the same.

"Hello, ladies."

Bess wove between her legs, her loud purr oozing with satisfaction as Jess obeyed and stroked her back.

"Have you had your dinner yet?" She glanced at the section of living room where four bowls sat empty. Either they had all eaten theirs already, or Vicky had stolen the other cats' food. There was a reason she was so plump. "Hmm. Neither have I."

She threw a heat-and-eat meal into the microwave then moved to the cupboard where the cat food was stashed, which instantly drew loud meows. So maybe she'd been so busy she hadn't fed them. What a bad mom she'd make, if she couldn't even remember feeding her fur-babies.

She spooned out their food, replenished their water, and watched them eat then scamper and play. Her heart eased a little. She needed this little pause. Needed a moment to let the other stuff fade into the background for a time. What would it be like to get off the mouse-wheel of work with its endless running, and just stop? Thus was the contradiction of a workaholic. One enjoyed working so then wanted to work, which often then meant saying yes to so many things that one *needed* to work, which didn't allow too much in the way of opportunity to just be. To breathe. Be still. To enjoy life, instead of feeling like she was forever hurtling to the next thing. No wonder her dad had needed stress leave. She'd read reports and statistics that showed veterinarians were among those who most often suffered mental stress thanks to the constant seesaw brought about by emotional investment and disappointment and being vilified by pet owners. There was a reason so many sought escape from the profession—sometimes, tragically, even from life.

Was that why Cooper had said what he had last year? Had he been worried about her?

Nope. Not thinking about him.

But… how would her life be different if she wasn't caught in the rat race of constant pressure? Who would she be if she wasn't Doc Martin, the local vet of Trinity Lakes and surrounds?

Seconds ticked away, as her thoughts tipped and swayed, the undercurrents brought to the surface last May begging for attention once again.

BOOM!

Sparks and smoke exploded from the microwave amid a screech of cat protests. She coughed, snatching a kitchen towel that she flapped furiously but vainly at the flames within.

The microwave was on fire? What was she supposed to do?

The smoke detector emitted piercing shrieks, sending the yowling cats through the cat flap to safety outside. "Come on, Jess, remember!"

Lord?

Clarity followed her micro prayer. Quick, she needed to turn off the power to stop the fan from fueling the fire with oxygen, then get the fire extinguisher.

She reached across to the microwave touchpad, but it was too hot. "Ow!"

She looked around. Where was the extinguisher, anyway? She couldn't see it, so grabbed the kitchen's fire blanket from the top kitchen cupboard and threw it over the microwave, which instantly cut the smoke emission by half. Then, above the persistent smoke alarm screeches, she heard a sound like the front door was getting a pummeling, and she yelled, "I'm back here."

A minute later her new next-door neighbor, Nick McDavid, appeared, his face pressed against the window. She hurried to unlock the back door and he rushed in. "You got a fire?"

She nodded, shaking, as she pointed to the smothered microwave. She usually did better with stressful situations than this.

He moved closer, shifting the blanket before stepping back quickly. "You didn't have an extinguisher?"

"I don't know where it is."

He shot her a look that said he'd heard the same excuse a score of times before. At least he didn't say it. "Well, if you can't find an extinguisher, then covering an electrical fire with a blanket is the next best thing to do. Looks like you did the right thing here. It's almost out."

She didn't normally appreciate being mansplained to, but given he was a new member of the local fire department, and a not unattractive—okay, extremely good-looking—single man in his early thirties, she wasn't about to go on a feminist rampage now.

"You all right?" he asked her.

She nodded, drawing in an unsteady breath, then suddenly started choking.

"Hey." He filled a glass of water from the sink and handed it to her, then moved to open the windows and door. "I know it's cold, but you gotta release the smoke so it doesn't stink up the whole house."

"Thanks." Her voice was croaky.

"Are your pets okay?"

"Oh my gosh, I forgot." See? She was such a bad mother. She rushed to the veterinary section of the house and tugged open the door. Then relaxed. This part of the building didn't even smell like smoke.

"Everything okay?" he called down the hall.

"Yeah."

The persistent screeches of the fire alarm suddenly stopped, and her shoulders slumped some more. How much damage had her moment of inattention done to the kitchen?

She arrived back to see Nick remove the fire-retardant blanket, then joined him in a wince.

"Was that dinner?" He gestured to the melted cardboard and plastic offering sitting black and forlorn on the glass turntable.

"Not anymore."

His mouth curved up a notch on one side. "Sorry. It's been a tough day, huh?"

"This was the cherry on top."

"You got something else to eat? You're welcome to share my dinner. It's just pizza, but it does the job."

Her heart thudded. Who needed a Dream Match when Mr. Dreamy was standing right in front of her? Then she shifted, catching a glimpse of herself in the glass cabinet, and gasped. Was that soot smeared across her face? And Nick hadn't said anything? No wonder he was taking pity on her, because clearly that was what he was doing. Because she was pitiable. Pitiful, even.

"Thanks," she managed to mutter. "But I need to clean up."

"Okay, then." He stepped back. "It's Jennifer, right?"

She cringed again. Also clear was the fact she hadn't made an impact on him the way he had on her. Although tonight was certainly memorable. "Jessica, actually."

"Well, you take care then, Jessica actually."

His crooked grin was enough to smother her inner eye-roll, and she coughed as she walked him to the door. "Thanks for coming to my rescue."

He saluted her. "I live to serve."

She smiled, her shoulders sagging as he walked from view. Awesome.

She wasn't hungry now—adrenaline still roared through her system, and seemed to have cut her hunger cues—and the smell of smoke made her nose wrinkle. She had to get out of these clothes and wash her hair. The cats would come inside when they were ready.

She made a half-hearted effort to call them in, then when they didn't come, closed the door. The house didn't need to get any colder than it already was. She shut the door to the kitchen and went down the hall to her bedroom, grabbed her night clothes and went to the bathroom.

Half an hour later, hair washed twice, she finally felt hungry enough to make a sandwich. She was so weary that she didn't trust herself to use any kitchen appliance. She finally plugged in her phone, which sprang to life with the dozens of notifications from before. Her nose wrinkled. She should probably contact her parents, let them know about her little kitchen mishap. But, given the hour, and the fact they were away for another ten days, they might not need to know. She could just buy a replacement microwave, and hopefully she could clean the kitchen of the smoke stains so they'd be none the wiser.

"None the *worried*," she muttered aloud. Of course, if they asked she'd tell them, but they didn't need their perfect vacation spoiled by her incompetence.

She scrolled through the other notifications, then saw the one from Dream Match. Her breath hitched, and she tapped on the screen. A pink cloud puff burst open with the words "You've got a Dream Match!"

She did? What was she going to say now? She sank onto the kitchen stool, peering at the now unblurred profile picture of the man who had seemed so right. Next door Nick, with his biceps and chiseled features, which probably equated to chiseled abs, might be dreamy but he wasn't exactly her type. A man that good looking probably needed to be with someone equally beautiful, and that so wasn't her. But this man, BizC, seemed to share a similar sense of humor to her, given his picture of a long distance shot of a man, his back to the camera, as he studied a mountain.

Her head tilted. Had she seen that mountain before? It reminded her of something. She rubbed her eyes. She must be imagining things. Anyway, what did that matter when the countdown was now on, and given the fact this match had happened eight hours ago, she now only had just under sixteen hours to respond before the match would dissolve. Which led straight back to the question of what she was going to ask him.

She exhaled. One of the things that set Dream Match apart was their focus on genuine applicants, which meant Dream Matchees agreed to make a move in that first day to prove their interest and stop time wasters. So she only had a limited time frame in which to respond, and the clock was counting down. It was part of what had appealed to her about this site, the fact that women were in control and could make the first move. Not only did it feel very twenty-first-century girl power, giving women the right to choose their destiny, but it also weeded out more of the creeps who stalked these places, or so the dating app's reviews had suggested. Still, she really should've thought through this stage of the process more.

She propped her head in her hands. "Lord, what do I say?"

Nothing sprang to mind, the weary whimpers of her day struggling to get past the intense weight of mental and physical exhaustion. It didn't matter. She had another—she checked the clock, wincing—fifteen hours and fifty-eight minutes to reply.

She should get some sleep. She could think about this tonight and respond first thing in the morning.

She put her phone down. Said goodnight to Anne and Bess who'd decided to slink in and curl up on their beds. Switched off lights. Set her alarm. Sank into deep, delicious sleep.

And slept past her alarm.

COOPER HURRIED past Travis's office, then went to clear out his desk. If he'd thought this through better yesterday, he would've done a more thorough retrieval of personal items, rather than leave it a day which meant he'd faced a brief verbal battle with security downstairs. But the shock that had taken him straight home meant he hadn't been thinking clearly. And once he'd been back in his apartment, he realized just how bare and stark it was and nothing like a real home. It was no wonder his siblings had called him out before on his hermit-like life, calling his apartment the equivalent of a cardboard box. Given that most of his furniture had come from IKEA he guessed that was fair.

"I thought you were sick," Tyson said.

Cooper fake-coughed. Yep, apparently he still had plenty of petty left inside. "That's why I'm leaving."

"I don't understand."

Nope, Tyson never had. About so many things.

He collected his stuff, said goodbye to a few of the weekend-working colleagues who he'd vaguely considered as friends, but when the geeks barely glanced up, he realized just how one-sided this whole deal had been. Exactly why had he stayed here for so long? Likely it had something to do with the big fat check burning a hole in his wallet.

He dumped his stuff in his Mercedes, next to his other things. He'd packed up what he wanted from his apartment and arranged with the building supervisor to rent out the space as a furnished home. He'd get more for rent that way.

Two hours later he was shooting north approaching Williams on Highway 5, most of his earthly possessions in the trunk of his convertible. Already he was regretting this car choice. It made sense in California with the sunny skies, but he could already guess the looks he'd get once he pulled into Trinity Lakes. He knew that Jackson's new wife Lexi had thought him a bit of a tool at first, even if his later actions had helped—he hoped—clear up that misunderstanding. He wasn't arrogant, but he made no apologies for liking nice things. He'd earned enough to be choosy. Or he had. He frowned.

His phone beeped a notification. He glanced at the car's in-dash screen. Frowned some more. Dream Match girl still hadn't contacted him, and there were only two hours to go until their dream match went bust. Did she not like his profile pic? He'd thought it kind of fun how they both had similar photos, but maybe that was too random for her, and she thought his lack of cheesy-grin-pic-with-dog made him a serial killer or something.

He tapped the leather steering wheel. This waiting for her to do something was killing him. Patience had never been his friend, and now he could barely cope while waiting for her to make the first move.

But really, how could he be thinking of trying to have a relationship when he'd just lost his job? That sure made him sound like a winner. His mouth flatlined. And he'd probably need to update his LinkedIn profile soon, before someone discovered he no longer worked for Manson IQ and reported him and he was booted from the website for fraud. That'd really go down well with someone who'd wanted honesty.

Except… if losing his job meant he didn't need to be based in California anymore, maybe he could pursue things. And if the lady wanted to meet in person he need not insist on having to stay close to home. And given there was no stipulation on when he got a new job, he might be able to get one straight away. Where he wanted. Where his dream match lived, if need be.

A sign post flashed past. One hundred miles to Redding. He'd need to fuel up there before the long tracts of forest swallowed up civilization. It'd be a long ten hours home from there, at least, but he liked driving. And doing this trip that would take him to east Washington via volcano country like Oregon's Crater Lake was so different from his usual speed that he might even enjoy the break. It would give time to think, to be still, even if he'd be pushing the speed limits and hoping no highway patrol cops were feeling the need to meet today's quota.

Yet sitting still also gave a little too much time to think. It was one thing to hope Ms. Dream Match would think him dreamy enough to message. It was another thing to go back and face the one he'd let get away.

Regret gnawed, as the reason for his big blow up back in Trinity Lakes drew back to mind. Back to the front of his mind, anyway, because regrets lived at the back, never too far away. He should've been kinder to her, less insistent it was his way or the highway, even if he'd only been trying to speak the truth from a place of care. He had cared. He still did, although he knew that she'd never believe him. He'd fumbled his explanations, while she'd pointed out his double standards. If she was to find out what had happened to him in losing his job she'd never let him live it down. And while he didn't want to lie, he also knew secrets had a way of coming out in Trinity Lakes, especially when his family was concerned. And given how close she was—or had been—to his family, it would only be a matter of time before she knew, and then saw him as the huge hypocrite he now knew himself to be.

So much for being honest.

But was saying he was on leave a lie? It *was* leave. As in, he'd left, so it was permanent leave. His nose screwed up. He didn't think that would pass the honesty test. Or the God one, either, for that matter.

Which reminded him. "Hey God, I know it's been a few, but I really need You to guide me. With a job. With my family. With this girl." Guilt stroked. "And that one, too."

Her face flashed. Green eyes, dark hair, infectious smile. Passion in her heart, and fire in her bones. There'd been times when he really thought he'd loved her. Only to discover they'd never really shared a vision for the future. Until maybe now.

His stomach tensed. What would she say if she saw him? Which she would—it was inevitable, seeing Trinity Lakes was a small town. How would he treat her? Would she question why he was back when he'd as good as told her his future was some-where else?

He wouldn't blame her for blaming him. He deserved it.

"God, help her forgive me. I know I was in the wrong." He swallowed. "I don't feel like I can move on with someone new until that's made right."

Which meant he'd need to do all he could to make things right. See her. Own his mistakes. Beg her forgiveness. Pray for God to bless her. Which was something he could do right now.

"Hey God, please bless her. Give her strength and peace and help her to find joy in the middle of all her busyness." He swallowed, then dared to finally pray the prayer that had haunted him since their fight. "And bless her by helping her find the man she deserves." Which clearly wasn't him.

His heart panged. Still, he'd learned some things, about himself, and what really was important in life. The past twenty-four hours had only reinforced that. She'd see he was a different man if she was to ever give him a second chance—

But no. No good would come of thinking about that. That ship had sailed, and he'd been left behind. Besides, maybe some-thing would come of this dream match. Even if the woman didn't seem nearly as eager as he was.

His phone beeped a new notification, which cut the music playing on the car's audio system. He glanced at the car's in-dash screen. His spirits sank. Nope. Only Jackson. He tapped to hear the voice message.

"What do you mean you're coming to stay?" Jackson sounded upset. "Lexi's on early shifts this week and she really needs to sleep, and really doesn't need to have you turning up at one in the morning."

Shoot. He'd forgotten Jackson's newlywed status. No wonder the dude wasn't happy with him showing up, even if Ellie and their mom lived with him and Lexi in the ranch's main house too. Well, too bad, so sad. As the ranch's financial manager, Cooper had every right to return to his family home and keep an eye on things from the comfort of his own bedroom. It was impressive how much he'd managed to direct things from California, but an eye on the ground wouldn't go astray. But he'd forgotten about Lexi's nursing shifts.

Despite their differences, he had quickly grown fond of the redheaded Aussie nurse, and was glad she'd joined their family last year. His oldest brother Dermott was the first Reilly sibling to marry, and he'd chosen well with single mom Mindy, and her son Brandon, and by all accounts was enjoying their life running Greener Gardens on the Independence Islands, off South Carolina. And his other siblings were doing okay too, with Ellie and Jasper finally moving their relationship from the friendship zone to something more, and Mitchell's permanent bevy of women, although Cooper suspected he had feelings for someone in particular. His lips twisted. Cooper thought she was *really* particular—her grandmother certainly was—and she might be a little too particular for poor Mitch.

Still. They were all doing pretty well on the relationship front, which was pretty amazing considering their loser of a father had bailed on Mom and his kids before Cooper had turned three. And while his siblings had all managed to find love the old-fashioned way, he wondered what they'd say about him being on Dream Match.

He pulled into Redding, did a pit and gas stop, grabbed some food, and returned to the car. He glanced at his phone. The app showed less than ten minutes remained. Which meant his dream match hadn't liked what she'd seen. His spirits sank some more. It was one thing to return to Trinity Lakes having been fired—excuse me, *restructured* from a job—but still holding the tantalizing hope of a future relationship. It was quite another to be rejected on all fronts.

Rejection. It didn't feel good to be the loser again. He'd been used to feeling that way back in the day when high school had prioritized sports and brawn over brains. Hence why Jackson and Mitchell had excelled, Jackson going to state for wrestling, and Mitch excelling in hockey so much he'd ended up scoring a scholarship several states away. He didn't blame plants-loving Dermott moving away. Cooper had done the same, except only two states away, not like Dermott, who had moved as far away as he possibly could in the lower forty-eight.

Another glance. Five minutes to go, then the dream match would dissolve. She obviously wasn't as eager as him. Still, he'd have to guess this was what was meant to be, and keep trusting God that the right woman would appear at the right time. Which meant this dream match wasn't his. God obviously had someone better in mind.

Would *she* ever want to pick up from—?

No. Thinking like that was stupid. Anyway, he was pretty sure Ellie had mentioned something in her last message about some hot new firefighter dude who'd moved next door to the Martins. Ellie had probably said that to make him jealous. He hadn't responded. He steered onto Interstate 5. In another hour or so he'd get to the town with the awesome name of Weed, then veer off to take Highway 97 that'd take him all the way through Oregon and then the Columbia River. He'd turn right, and in another three hours he'd be home.

His phone dinged. He glanced at it. Then immediately steered onto the verge.

His pulse picked up. She'd left it to literally the last minute, the dying seconds, but she'd responded. He tapped the screen, and stared at her message.

BizC.

CHAPTER THREE

A surge of adrenaline spiked as Jess saw her message was marked as *Read*.

After sleeping past her alarm and rushing to work, and then finally finding a spare minute crammed with doubt and second guessing every single thing about this, she'd finally found the lamest thing beyond a simple "Hi" to say.

She bit her lip. What would he do? Now she'd opened the conversation, there were no time restrictions anymore. He could reply, or not. But seeing she'd stuck her neck out, she really hoped he'd say something back soon.

A pink cloud suggested a message was coming, then, poof! His message appeared.

Bless Bess.

She laughed. Okay. That was fair. Let's see if he really did share her sense of humor. *Bold of you to assume my name is Bess.*

Would he get it?

Ha ha. You're cute.

Her heart warmed. Yes, she really should be scrubbing down walls and wiping down the kitchen ceiling to remove smoke stains, but this was too much fun. Besides, the hardest-working vet in Trinity Lakes needed a coffee break. Even if it was two hours past when she usually aimed to re-caffeinate. And a Saturday, which was supposed to be a half day, although she'd already said yes to several more visits after this, in an attempt to catch up on her workload. That fact made her shoulders slump, as she refocused on the conversation that already was proving to be the brightest spot in her day.

Thank you, she typed.

You're welcome.

She smiled. So the guy did banter. She liked that. It reminded her of—nope. Not thinking about him. He was her past and Mr. BizC of Dream Match might very well be her future. She hoped.

I gotta run, he typed, *but looking forward to chatting more tomorrow.*

Excellent. Talk then. She signed off with a smiley face, second guessed the smiley face, then smiled as he sent a smiley face of his own.

Her heart fluttered. Oh, Mr. BizC, this could be fun.

SUNDAY ARRIVED, and Jess drove into the church parking lot and exited Big Red with a slam of the creaky door. Most of the congregation members at Trinity Life Church were used to her, but a few looked over with startled expressions, as if wondering why someone would dare show up to services in jeans, boots, and a ponytail, and drive a big red truck. Simple. It was for the same reason she tended to sit at the back in case her phone buzzed. She had to be ready to leave at a moment's notice. Which was why she didn't do the whole makeup and dress and heels things like some people did. Like Lexi Reilly, Jackson's new wife, who always had a bit of an Audrey Hepburn vibe about her, looking cool and classy and elegant. These days Georgia Darcy seemed to hold a similar personal aesthetic, as if the tomboy of two years ago had been chased away by going to college.

She greeted Mr. Carrigan, who was on the welcome team today, and slipped into the back row, before noticing a buzz near where the Reilly family sat. Her heart hitched. No. That couldn't be... Why was *he* here?

She shrank in her seat, hoping he wouldn't turn and see her, while also wishing she'd bothered to put makeup on to hide the shadows under her eyes. It was one thing to go for the natural look, to want to be seen as real, but it was quite another for an ex to see her and think she was falling apart. Which she *wasn't*. She straightened—a slumped posture sure wouldn't help dismiss that particular notion—and tilted her chin, taking care to look on the other side of the church, offering quick smiles to those who glanced her way. See? Not concerned. Not bothered at all that the man who'd basically shouted at her in the middle of Trinity Lakes had turned up unexpectedly for only the second time since that infamous moment last May.

It had to be unexpected, right? Neither Ellie nor Jackson had mentioned anything the other day, and Ellie surely wouldn't have been asking Jess about him if she'd known he was about to visit. Ugh. She was *so* over how Cooper Reilly managed to get inside her thoughts, stealing attention from God, no less!

She forced her attention to the front, but even though the worship and preaching was good, part of her kept counting down until the post-service meet-and-greet over coffee and cupcakes in the hall. Maybe she could invent an excuse. Although she probably wouldn't need an excuse, given the long list of things she needed to do, starting with finishing off cleaning the kitchen, which last night's late hour had put paid to.

The last song finished, and she joined the exodus, nearly bumping into a tall figure. "Oh! Sorry."

Nick McDavid smiled. "Howdy neighbor."

She couldn't decide whether he was being ironic with the clichés or not, but decided for the sake of friendly relations to not call him on it. The previous tenants had complained about the barking from the Martin property, even despite the fact they'd known they were moving next door to a vet clinic. City folk. Honestly. "How are you settling in?"

"Good enough." He glanced around. "It's pretty quiet in Trinity Lakes, huh?"

She fought a desire to be offended. "We find plenty to do, but winter isn't exactly known for being the peak season for activity."

"Hey, your life seems pretty exciting." His grin widened. "Did you get everything cleaned up?"

"Not yet," she admitted. "I had some visits to make, and haven't yet found the time."

He nodded. "If you need a hand, I'm happy to help."

"Aren't you on call?"

"I've had four days off, and I'm back tomorrow, so I can help today if you like." His lips twitched. "I'm a little taller than you, after all."

"True." She grinned back at the man standing nearly a foot taller than her.

A cleared throat swung her attention to the side, where Ellie stood.

Ellie's eyebrows rose as she glanced between Jess and Nick. "Pardon me for interrupting."

Jess's cheeks heated. "Oh, you're not…"

Ellie's glance showed skepticism then she held out her hand to Nick. "Hi, I'm Ellie Reilly."

"Nick McDavid." They shook.

"You're the new firefighter, right?"

"News travels fast."

"Wasn't me." Jess held up her hands.

"No. I think I heard Rhonda Ingalls say something." Ellie

studied her, like she was wondering why Jess hadn't said anything.

Like she had time to explain every single thing that occurred. Like she owed her friend any kind of explanation. Nick wasn't a secret. She just hadn't got around to telling her friends about him yet. Not that there was anything to tell. He lived next door. That was all.

"We're next door neighbors," Nick said, pointing to Jess.

"I know." Ellie sent Jess another pointed look.

"What?"

"So, excuse me Nick," Ellie smiled sweetly, "but I wanted a word with my friend here."

"Sure."

Ellie drew Jess aside. "You have some explaining to do," she murmured.

"There's nothing to say," she protested.

"Oh yes, there is. Did you see who is back?"

She could play dumb, or…

"You have." Ellie nodded with obvious satisfaction. "It was a total surprise. Apparently—"

Jess was jostled from behind, and she turned, all attempts at good humor draining away at the sight of the dark eyes. She stiffened. Willed her features to appear pleasant. Willed her heart and mouth to behave.

Cooper nodded. "Jess."

Her stomach dropped. That was it? Not even a hello? Fine. "Cooper." She glanced back at Ellie who watched them with a knit brow, and raised her eyebrows.

"Um, Cooper," Ellie said, grasping his arm, "Have you met Jess's new neighbor, Nick?"

"Nope." He nodded, and the men shook hands.

Jess swallowed. There was no contest in the looks department. Nick would win every time. He had the height, the chiseled features, styled hair and muscles that filled three million novels as exactly what a handsome hero should look like. But she'd always found Cooper's floppy dark hair and slim wiry build more her cup of chai. Until she'd learned just how dark was the heart that lay within.

"What do you do, Cooper?" Nick asked.

"I work in tech. You?"

"I'm with the Trinity Lakes fire department."

"Of course you are," Cooper muttered.

She didn't look at him, her earlier goal of pretending she wasn't bothered by his return and nearness having long curled up and died.

"It's a good thing, too," Nick said, crossing his arms so his biceps bulged. Did the man not notice the cold? Maybe having that many muscles gave an extra layer of insulation.

"Why do you say that?" Cooper challenged.

Well, it sounded like a challenge. Maybe she wasn't quite the nonentity to him he was pretending.

Nick glanced at her. "You haven't told your friends?"

Friend, she thought but didn't say. She shrugged and found an expression for Ellie she hoped conveyed nonchalance. "I had a little emergency on Friday night, and Nick was kind enough to come by and help me out."

Ellie's blue eyes grew enormous. "You had a fire?"

"Were you okay?"

Cooper's question earned him the quickest skim of a glance before she refocused on Ellie. "Just a small one, in the microwave. It stank out the house, though."

"Oh my goodness! *Are* you okay?" Ellie demanded.

"Fine and dandy."

"I'm going to help clean up this afternoon," Nick said, with a lift of his chin at Cooper. Huh, she'd seen that action before. For a second they'd worn the same look she'd seen between dueling bulls.

"I don't think she likes help," Cooper murmured, with his

own crossed arms.

"Excuse me?" She joined the arms brigade but with her hands on her hips as she turned to face Cooper. "What would you know?"

He studied her, and in his eyes she could read unhappiness. Well, tough. This mess between them was all of his own making.

She glanced away. "Excuse me. I need to speak to Jodie over there."

Because a second longer in Cooper's company felt like an hour too long. She needed to speak to somebody else—anybody else—for her own sanity.

She checked in on Jodie, and was nearly back to pre-Cooper-interaction calm when her arm was touched. Ellie again. "Have you got a minute?"

No. But the truth wasn't going to cut it with her friend. "Sure."

"What's going on with you?" Ellie hissed, when they were back in the main church building.

"Me?" She feigned nonchalance. "I don't know what you mean."

"Yes, you do. Come on. Give."

"There's nothing to give."

"Yes, there is. Spill the tea, girl. What's this about a fire and a hot firefighter?"

"Do you mean Nick?"

Ellie rolled her eyes at the stupid question.

"Look, I have to admit that was a little unexpected. He did show up—I think it was the smoke alarm that did it, it was so loud—but I certainly didn't ask him to come over and help today."

"Then why is he?"

"I don't know. Maybe he's a nice guy? He's just moved here, so I guess he might be lonely."

Ellie waggled her eyebrows. "Well, you could do something about that."

What? The thought a handsome firefighter might be interested in her, along with her mysterious Dream Match BizC, seemed impossible. She wasn't the girl guys sought. But given that BizC had swiped right and had kept the conversation going which suggested he did seem interested, perhaps it wasn't so impossible after all. "Maybe."

"Definitely! Come on. I know Cooper was unkind to you, but it doesn't mean all guys are the same."

A sharp rush of tears forced her to look away and bite her lip.

"If it makes any difference, I think he's sorry," Ellie said softly.

Jess shrugged, her words stolen by the emotion balling her throat. She really needed to move on.

"And call me crazy, but it looked like the two of them were prepared to arm wrestle over you."

Her lips twitched up. "You thought that?" *Too*, she mentally added.

"Come on," Ellie scoffed. "I know you thought that as well. And hey, it doesn't hurt to let a guy know he's not the only one out there."

Maybe so, but did that mean Cooper still cared for her? But if so, why hadn't he said anything to her? But no. She couldn't go down this track again. She'd wasted too many months last year doing exactly that, and all it had achieved was a thoroughly battered heart. When a girl couldn't trust someone whom she'd known all her life, who could she trust? She might as well trust an internet stranger. Like BizC.

Oh.

Ellie was looking at her seriously, and her skin prickled. She had to say something to prove to Cooper's sister that she was completely over him. Which she was. She tilted her chin. "Well, I'm not sure I like the idea of being someone to fight over."

"Why not? It proves that you've got—or you are—something they want." Ellie smiled. "Besides, it'd give you something to do other than spend all your life working, working, working."

"I'm not that bad."

"You actually kind of are." Concern laced Ellie's words.

"I do stuff for fun too."

"Like what?" Ellie challenged.

She bit her lip. Was now the time to confess about her dream match? But it was all too new, and there'd been basically nothing but the briefest of exchanges, so it was probably best to not say anything yet. Not until there was something more to tell.

"I gotta go."

"No, you don't get out if it that easily. What are you up to?"

For maybe the first time in her life she blessed her phone's interruption. She drew it from her back pocket, glanced at the number, and winced. "Sorry. I need to take this."

"Just remember, all work and no play make Jessica a dull girl."

"Thanks, Ellie. Appreciate it."

"Any time." Ellie hugged her. "Have some fun, okay?"

"Yes, ma'am." Jess tapped the screen to answer the call. "Hello, Mr. Walker, is it your goats again?"

———

COOPER WATCHED JESS LEAVE, her tall fireman dude following mere seconds later. His heart wrenched. Why had he acted like such a jerk instead of saying exactly what he'd spent half of yesterday's trip planning to say?

Because of the fireman dude, standing there, looking at Jess like she was his for the asking. Well, no thanks. Not under his watch.

"So, what brings Cooper Reilly back to the fold?" Pastor Theo Ladan asked.

"I'm taking some leave," he hedged. Was lying to a church minister worse than lying to a normal person? Not that Theo wasn't normal. It just felt like he had a shortcut to God.

"And how long are you in town for?"

"I'm not sure." Not when he needed a new job, and hoped to finally sort things with Jess, and delve into exploring whether the promising start with BlessBess would allow for something more. "A few weeks, at least."

"I see."

For a strange second Cooper thought he did.

"Well, any time you want to talk, you know where I am."

"Thanks."

He kinda liked how the man didn't pussyfoot around him. He spoke straight, with none of the bulldust he'd gotten used to with the likes of Tyson or Travis from work. He winced. His *former* work.

"Everything okay?"

He nodded. "It will be. Excuse me."

He hugged his mom, said he'd see her at home, offered a hand of farewell to Jasper Cohen and Josh Ladan, and escaped into the cold outside. Just in time to see Jess drive past in Big Red. She glanced at him but didn't smile, and his heart twisted again. What was it she'd said? She had a fire in her kitchen? He could—should—would *definitely* go help her clean up, then finally make the grand apology he should've made last May instead of watching her walk away.

But how exactly was he supposed to apologize for caring about someone and not wanting to see them burn out? He was darned if he apologized, darned if he didn't. Still, he had to make a start.

He drove there, but Big Red wasn't in the drive. But Hot Firedude was, cleaning off his car as if giving the local neighbors a private show.

"Hey, Connor, wasn't it?"

"Cooper." Jerk. "Is Jess in?"

Fireman Sam shook his head. "She had to go to a job." He lifted his brows. "Something I can help you with?"

"Nope. Thanks."

Fine. He'd come back later.

Maybe he'd see if his brother and sister were at Joe's Diner. He could do with an easy chat.

But when he got there, it was to see four cozy couples: Jackson and Lexi, Ellie and Jasper, Josh and Hallie, and Brandon and Jodie. Memories of how he and Jess had once fitted in drew fresh regret, and instead of joining them, he ordered food to-go instead.

"You're not staying?" Jasper asked.

"Sorry. Had a huge drive yesterday, and need to catch some Zzz's." He fake-yawned. Oh, look at him, actor extraordinaire. California had rubbed off on him. "But we'll catch up soon."

"You're around for a while?" Josh asked.

Cooper wondered how much Josh shared with his father and vice versa. "A little while."

"He's being very mysterious," Ellie announced.

"What are you doing in town anyway?" he asked her. "I thought you had college or something."

She shrugged, then turned to Jasper with a smile. "I did, but I took Friday off for Valentine's Day, seeing this was my first with a real sweetie."

Jasper's face brightened, and he leaned in and kissed Ellie, which drew smiles and laughter from the others. Not him. He might fake-smile, but he just knew regret. If he hadn't messed up things he too might've been sitting with the woman of his dreams. But Jess had clearly moved on with her handsome fire-fighter dude.

Marlene called that his order was ready so he grabbed at the excuse and left. Only to go to the park near Wainscott Lake and eat his Trinity burger and drink his chocolate shake—some of his small-town roots had never left—and stare at the gray sheath of water. How long would Jess be? Should he maybe go there and surprise her by cleaning up whatever needed cleaning himself? But she'd never liked surprises, or people speaking for her, which was why he'd objected at church when Fireman Dan, or whatever his name was, started getting all controlling.

He glanced at his phone, sorely tempted to get back on Dream Match and initiate the next conversation. But leaving things so unfinished between him and Jess felt wrong, and he really wanted to sort that out before going ahead with anything new.

He opened the app, saw that BlessBess hadn't written anything new either, and smiled at their matching smile emojis. Sure, it might be a little childish, but he liked that she felt open like that with him, wasn't trying for a cool he wasn't into either.

Which made him wonder…

He scrolled through his phone and found a joke and sent it. He hoped she liked it, and that she knew it meant he was thinking of her. He'd try to message her tonight, and maybe they'd even talk, so he could hear her voice. Then again, taking things slow would probably be for the best. Seeing he hadn't even seen a proper picture of her yet, there was no point in chasing a real conversation. Besides, this flirting by messages was fun.

Another glance at the time pushed him to his feet. Surely Jess had to be back home by now. And he hadn't been joking before. After his big drive yesterday he was tired, and he did need a sleep, even though he was fairly sure that put him into grandpa territory. So he wanted to see Jess now, then he could return to the Reilly Ranch and grab a nap, instead of going there and coming back to town again.

He disposed of his trash and moved back to his car, and steered it back to Wainscott Drive and the Martin clinic. Big Red was parked out the front. His heart eased, then thudded. Okay, so this was it. She was here, he would finally speak to her and apologize.

He knocked on the front door, and prayed she'd be open to hearing him. Surely she'd be expecting an apology, even though this was much, much later than what she was entitled to.

He knocked again, and smiled as the door was flung open. But not by Jess. Instead it was her fireman dude.

"You again."

His smile dropped away. "You again too." Ugh. How lame did he sound? "Uh, is Jessica here?" His heart tensed. Of course she was. She had to be. Otherwise how had this dude got in? How he hated having to play second fiddle to some random stranger. "Jess?" he called, then moved in.

"Whoa." Fire-dude placed a palm on Cooper's shoulder. "What do you think you're doing?"

"I'm going to speak to her." He glanced at the hand. "Get your hand off me."

"Touchy, huh? Well, how about we find out if Jess wants to speak to you?"

"Excuse me? Who made you her guardian?"

Fireman Stan lifted his massive square jaw. "I'm looking out for my neighbor, and when a random guy tries to push his way inside her house, I'm not going to let him."

"Random guy? I'm not the random guy here." Cooper glared, and tapped his own chest. "I'm the one who was her friend all through high school, all through college. I'm definitely not the random dude here."

"Cooper?" Jess's voice swung their attention her way.

"Hey, Jess." He inched away from firefighter dude. Best he

didn't give her a reason to compare the pair of them anytime soon. The man probably had his own calendar somewhere.

"What are you doing here?" Jess frowned.

"I know you're busy, so I, uh, came to see if you needed help cleaning up."

"Cleaning up? From what?"

"Um, a little thing called a fire yesterday?" How could she have forgotten? How often did a person have a fire?

"That was on Friday night," Fire Model said.

"I'm talking to Jess, here," Cooper gritted out.

"I can see that." He folded his beefy arms across his chest.

Man. Did he practice that pose in the mirror? Probably, for all the calendars he'd been asked to pose for.

Jess sighed. "Excuse us, Nick—"

So that was his name.

"This won't take long."

Oh. Cooper's heart sank. Judging from that comment, any attempt at apology didn't seem like it would be received with open arms.

Nick nodded, eyeing Cooper with a narrowed gaze, as if to say watch it, buster.

Indignation roiled within. Who did he think he was?

"Well?" Jess asked, her arms folded.

She was so pretty, her hair sliding out of her ponytail, even with a smudge of dirt on her nose.

"Well, Cooper? I don't have all day."

"You know you have dirt on your nose?" Whoa. Way to go with the smooth apology. "I mean—"

She touched her nose. "You came here to say that?"

"No. I came to see if you needed help cleaning up after the fire, and—"

"Why?"

"What do you mean why? Because I wanted to help, and I know you're busy and might need an extra hand."

"Are you serious?"

"One hundred percent." Wait. Judging from her scowl she didn't mean that in a hopeful way.

"This is the first thing you say to me in nearly a year?"

"Technically, I think I said 'Merry Christmas' last year," he tried to joke.

"No, you didn't."

He hadn't?

"So the first thing you do is say I'm too busy—again—and now you think I want your help?"

"Wait, that wasn't what I meant."

She grabbed the door and began closing it. "I don't need your help. I have someone here who already offered, and is way nicer than you proved to be."

"Jess, come on. Please hear me out."

"You said that to me once before, and I stayed and listened, and I've regretted it ever since."

Was that a sparkle of tears in her eyes? He stepped forward. "Jess, I'm sor—"

"You heard her dude." Nick scowled from behind her. "You better scram before I call the cops."

"Are you freakin' kidding me?" He looked back at Jess. "I just wanted to talk."

She shook her head. "You have nothing to say that I want to hear."

And with that she slammed the door in his face.

CHAPTER FOUR

Jess's fingers trembled, but she couldn't let Nick see how much Cooper's unexpected visit had rattled her. "Would you mind making coffee? I need the bathroom for a moment."

She exited the hall without waiting for an answer, then went and sat on the edge of the bath, her hands covering her face to stop the moisture threatening to leak from her eyes. Oh, she'd handled that so badly. She should've just told Cooper to apologize, but his stupid comment about dirt on her face had tipped her over the edge and back into resentment. What did he think she was supposed to look like, when she'd been scrubbing out cupboards? At least Nick hadn't said anything about how bad she looked. But for that to be the first real thing Cooper had said to her in nearly a year...

Breath shuddered in and out. She was so tired of this tension, so tired of carrying it in her heart. Each time she thought she was over it something pricked its ugly head to rise again, and she was left trying to beat it into submission. She sucked in a shaky breath.

A tap came on the door. "You okay in there?"

"Yep!" Her lie echoed off the tiles.

God bless Nick. God bless him for helping her out, for his protectiveness, for proving to be a distraction from the man she didn't want taking up space in her thoughts. See, here was a man she could like. Ellie was right, and from all that she'd learned in the past hour as he'd helped, the man was very much single. But—her heart sank—apart from his faith it seemed they had little else in common. One of the things she'd always liked about Cooper was his wit, and so far that appeared lacking in Nick. But what good was wit when it accompanied rudeness? Although maybe she'd been a bit too quick to judge...

Two hours later, she'd thanked Nick for his help, promising him a dinner as thanks on Friday night, and could finally breathe a sigh of relief. It was getting dark outside, and the house might smell of Clorox but at least it didn't hold the smoke stains of before.

Bess rubbed against her legs. The other cats didn't seem to like the smell much either, and were still outside, but she didn't mind. After the day she'd endured—along with scrubbing kitchens and managing men and poor Mr. Walker's goats, one of whom had needed to be euthanized—she finally had the chance to relax. She opened the Dream Match app. Saw BizC had left a cartoon. It made her smile for the first time in forever.

Of course, that sparked a hunt for her own funny meme, and she posted one of a cat eating ice cream. Not something any vet who cared about the welfare of their animal would permit, but it was funny nonetheless.

She wondered if he'd message more, and she ate her sandwich—she'd planned to buy a new microwave today but Mr. Walker's call had prevented that—and closed her eyes. She was so tired. Eating on the sofa wasn't Mom's idea of good housekeeping, but seeing Mom wasn't here, she'd never know.

Her head lolled. She really should check on the cats, but she was too tired. How had Dad managed all these years? It must've helped to have had Mom manage the administration side of things, but even with the automated scheduling systems Jess had put in place eighteen months ago—thanks to Cooper's expertise and assistance—she felt like she was running on empty. Maybe her iron levels were low or something.

Or maybe she needed to start taking weekends off, like Cooper, and yes, Ellie and others, had advised in recent years. But just because she might schedule time off didn't mean the work would stop. Animals didn't consult her diary and make better plans for when they needed help. And she needed to help. Her heart beat to help animals, and it killed her when they suffered. So while it might be nice to say she needed time off, she couldn't really do so. Especially as she was one of the only vets in the area. If she took time off, the job list would only compound, and then how could she possibly keep up?

A headache pounded, and she pressed deep into her skull to keep it away. Her phone buzzed with a message. She glanced at the name on the screen. Cooper.

Her heart tensed, and she swiped to delete it. No way. She couldn't deal with him just yet. Couldn't deal with anything he had to say. Look how well she'd dealt with the last thing he'd tried to say.

Regret gnawed. To his credit, he had appeared contrite. And it wasn't his fault that she'd been anxious and hurting after having to euthanize a foolish goat with a wanderlust. Tears sparked, her throat tightening. Maybe she should have seen what he said.

She retrieved the message from the trash and read it. Her eyes watered more.

I'm sorry for everything I've done to hurt you. Please forgive me. I feel so bad. I wish we could be friends again.

Friends? Was he kidding?

But then, the realization drifted softly that he'd done exactly what she'd wanted and apologized. Not in person like she'd hoped, although a tiny part of her wondered if that was why he'd called around, and been scared off by Nick.

She didn't blame Nick for being over-protective. He was only doing what any first responder worth their salt would do, as he'd explained once she'd returned from the bathroom. But it made her wonder just what Cooper would've said if given half a chance.

Bess leapt onto the corner of the couch and eyed her solemnly.

"You think I should forgive him?"

Bess blinked once then licked her paw. She'd take that as a yes.

She studied Cooper's message again. Forgiveness she might do, especially because his third sentence seemed genuine. But that last request? She wasn't sure she could ever trust the man who'd stolen then broken her heart. She might forgive him, but trust him?

"Jesus, what do I do?" she prayed aloud.

The answer was plain, so she typed and sent it: *Forgiven.* But definitely not forgotten. And she wasn't ready to explore friend-ship with him any time soon.

She muted his number so any further messages begging for friendship would remain unseen. She didn't have the emotional capacity for that right now. Forgiveness felt big enough.

But she did have enough emotional capacity for silly memes.

She flicked open the Dream Match app and saw BizC was composing something. A puff of pink smoke appeared, followed by his words.

How was your day?

She pressed her lips together. Sure, she had people around her who cared, but this private inquiry felt special, like he really wanted to know.

It had its moments, she typed back.

Some good ones I hope?

Yep. There'd been a few. Like church. And Nick's offer of help. And Cooper's message. She swallowed. *How about you?*

Same.

She stroked Bess's ginger hair, wondering what to say next. This whole getting to know someone new felt strange. There was a world of questions out there: likes, dislikes, interests, food preferences, favorite places. Where did one begin?

The dots began rolling, signaling he was composing his next message.

I got something resolved today that had bothered me forever, so I felt like I had a win.

That's a good feeling, she typed back.

Right?

She sent back a smiley face.

She wondered whether he'd had that revelation in church today, then wondered how much church and God and faith even factored in his life. He'd said they did on his profile—that was one of the ways they were a dream match—but how much did following Jesus really matter to him?

But digging into matters of personal belief felt a little intrusive when they hadn't even discussed favorite foods. What was something innocuous she could ask to keep the conversation rolling?

The muted hockey game on TV flickered light over the living room. *What did you last binge watch on TV?*

His answer came soon: *I've been working so hard lately that I haven't binge-watched anything for years, but I know I need to relax more, so I'm planning for that to change.*

Huh. *Ditto.*

Their exchanges continued, until she asked if he was watching anything now.

His reply came back immediately: *Okay, it's not very romantic, but I'm watching hockey.*

Me too! she typed. *Go Minnesota.*

You follow hockey?

Only that team. I know the family of one of the players.

She stared at that last sentence, then deleted it, letter by letter, until only the first sentence remained. Owning up to too much truth felt like it had the potential to pierce this cozy bubble of anonymity. And while she hadn't owned up to what state she lived in, let alone Trinity Lakes, she had said she lived in the Pacific Northwest, so that would narrow it down somewhat. There were only a few handfuls of players born in the PNW, so chances were Mitchell Reilly might be a name that BizC would recognize. And she didn't want to get side-tracked with discussion around Mitchell. Not when she'd rather BizC focus on her. She pressed send.

His reply came a moment later, as if he'd been waiting for hers. *Me too.*

Her heart thudded. How many things did they have in common? It seemed insane that of all the people that would meet they would both be watching hockey at the same time, and both be following the same team. And sure, it was early days yet, but it fueled hope that maybe this was not just a match orchestrated by some tech company's special algorithms, but that maybe God had a hand in it too.

The back and forth kept going, as they commented on everything from plays to ads to music tastes, and she realized just how tricky this tightrope between anonymous sharing and honesty could be. It probably was a good thing they weren't meeting in person any time soon, as he'd probably be able to read her, given her face couldn't hide a thing. And yet one day they would—obviously—have to meet, if this progressed as she hoped and prayed it might.

But for right now, that was something she'd happily put off for as long as she could. Because flirting like this, exchanging opinions and discovering shared values and just how many other things they had in common, felt safe, felt good, like slipping into a warm pair of flannel PJs as it snowed outside. She was comfortable, like she'd once been with Cooper. Her heart panged. And while that friendship would likely never recover, this online messaging with BizC made her feel like the world didn't have to end with a friend's betrayal. He might have apologized, and she might have forgiven him, but it didn't mean she could trust him. This messaging with BizC fueled hope that there were good guys out there still.

She stretched, smiling at a hockey meme he sent, as the edges of her heart toyed with something that felt a little like contentment. Because lying here, feeling the most relaxed she had in weeks, if not months, showed just how much she valued feeling important to someone. That while some relationships had passed their best-by date, there still remained potential for something more. Maybe even something better. *Please Lord.*

PLEASE LORD, *I need a job.* After arriving late Saturday night—or had his arrival at the ranch nudged Sunday morning?—he'd spent the past five days exhausting his sparse knowledge of ranch things while tweaking the websites of both the ranch and ranch stay, checking the financials, and dodging questions about the nature of his "leave." Yes, he didn't love not admitting to the full truth, but figured it'd be easier for his family if he had another job to go to. Especially his mom. Jackson was focused on the ranch and Brutus's efforts as the baby daddy for most of the county's calves—when he wasn't focused on Lexi, that was. Ellie had a finger in a million pies it seemed, between her studies, her work at the ranch, coordinating the ranch stays with Mom, and overseeing the Trinity Lakes historical museum. When she wasn't planning her wedding, discussing details with Mom, either in person, as she had before returning to Seattle early Tuesday morning, or via video call.

Mom was simply glad to have him home. And it was good to be here for an extended period of time and see just how well she was doing now. When their dad had left back when he was three, she'd taken on running the ranch, and raising five kids, the youngest, Ellie, just a baby. And while Mom might've had Denny Graham's help with running the ranch, she'd run the family mostly herself, especially after her parents-in-law had died soon after their son disappeared.

Disappeared Donald Reilly had, and he'd been declared legally dead these past many years. And while Donald's demise meant nothing to him—how could he regret a man he couldn't remember who had walked out on his young family?—he did regret how his father's absence had worn their mother down. She'd gotten sick a couple of years ago, when Lexi's nursing skills had really come to the fore, and she'd slowly recovered from her bedridden state. And seeing things like Jackson finding a wife, and Ellie falling in love, had helped bring her back to the mother he remembered. He'd told Mom a million times he'd pay for a cleaner or do what he could to make her life easier. But she was as stubborn as the rest of them—hence why she'd never sold the ranch—and she'd refused. So being here, spending time with her, was comforting for both of them, especially as the rest of the world seemed to keep rolling on by without them.

His mom glanced at him as she washed up. She barely used the dishwasher unless the house was full of guests, thinking it used more water. Which might be true, but he'd never done the environmental math like Liam and Elissa Darcy next door, so he couldn't know for sure.

"Can I do something for you, Mom?" he asked.

She smiled. "Look who's getting all domesticated."

"Yeah, not quite." He took a sip of coffee.

Her brow arched. "Have you got a special someone in your life?"

He choked on his coffee. "Mom."

"Is that a no, then?"

"What is it with mothers wanting to see their kids settling down?" he complained.

"I just want my children to be happy."

"I am happy."

She studied him with the same cool look that Ellie had too, like she could see through the smoked glass of his façade. "You're not happy, son. What's wrong?"

His lips pressed together, and he shook his head.

"I can't help but feel that something isn't right, Cooper."

He exhaled. Maybe it was time to admit things. "I'm thinking about a new job."

"You're not enjoying where you're at?"

Man up. Tell her. "I've left Manson."

Her eyes widened. "You didn't say that before."

"I didn't know how to."

"Well, you say it like that, son."

Yeah. Apparently.

"So you need a new job." Mom's brow puckered. "Is that what's worrying you?"

"One day. I actually got a really good payout, so I'm not in any hurry."

She nodded. "Best to find the right one rather than rush in and get it wrong."

The way she said that, he wondered if she meant more than just a job.

"Is that what's bothering you? Or is it something else?"

It was kind of scary the way his mom could read him.

"Did you ever make things up with Jessica?"

Tightness formed in his chest. *Lord, bless Jess.* "I thought I had."

"Meaning?"

He confessed his Sunday afternoon debacle, finishing with "at least she said she's forgiven me."

"You don't believe her?"

His throat grew raw. "She didn't say she wanted to be my friend." Saying it like that made him sound like a preschooler, but it was the reality, and the rawness of that still hurt, digging away at his defenses. "I want to make things up to her, but I don't think she'll ever forgive me."

"It was embarrassing for her, Coop. You got to leave but she had to stay here and suffer a hundred nosy inquiries from the likes of Rhonda Ingalls."

He winced. He could just imagine how that went.

"She's a tough cookie, but you know her. She doesn't find it easy to hedge around the truth, so I think she must've found it very hard to try to stop people putting the full blame on you when she didn't know why you said what you did."

"She didn't blame me?"

"Oh, I think she did, but she didn't want everyone in Trinity Lakes despising you, so she was very careful about what she said. And I imagine that was hard, especially when she didn't understand your reasons."

His mom was the only person he'd explained things to. That he'd been worried about Jess and her insane workload, and was growing increasingly concerned that she was taking on too much. His mom had understood his reasons, had even said she'd felt the same, but she'd pointed out his lack of wisdom in confronting her on the main street on a day which should've been focused on the opening of Ellie's museum.

"That was the sort of conversation that needs to happen in private, son."

"I was just caught in the moment," he mumbled.

"I know. You wanted her best, and thought she'd see a future with you."

"And now I think she wants a future with her fireman neighbor."

His mother's nose wrinkled. "Oh dear."

Exactly.

"Well, you can't predict how these things will work out," she said matter-of-factly. "And just because something may appear to be a certain way doesn't mean it will stay like that."

Her face dimmed, and he wondered if she was thinking about her marriage. What must it have been like to just have your husband walk out, leaving you with all the debts and cares and responsibilities? He'd never forgive his father for doing that to his mom.

"Pray for her, son."

"I am," he admitted hoarsely. *Lord, bless her.*

"You're a good boy."

He blinked, hard, thankful that his brothers weren't here to see him get teary. Man. He really needed a job. Hanging out in the kitchen like this was messing with his testosterone levels.

His phone beeped. Dream Match. Bless Bess had sent a new message.

He smiled at the cat picture, and wondered for the hundredth time just where she lived. He liked the sense of mystery, but was also getting impatient to know when they could meet. They obviously had so many things in common and he wanted to know more. What did she look like? What was her voice like? He was glad that Dream Match didn't emphasize superficial things, and it might've only been less than a week, but there was a limit to how long a man could wait without wondering if his potential girlfriend was pretty.

He bet she was pretty. At night he liked to imagine what she looked like. With that dark hair she might be Latino, or even Asian. He could imagine an exotic beauty, even if he wasn't sure how someone from a different culture might fit into his white bread ranching family. But finding a way to get her to send a picture without looking shallow was going to require thought.

"What are you smiling about?"

He peered up at his mom. While she might know most of the truth about his falling out with Jess, she might not be ready to hear about this. "Just a crazy cat picture."

He showed her, taking care to obscure the Dream Match logo with his thumb.

Mom smiled. "I think I've seen a cat like that before."

"It's a ginger cat, Mom. They're everywhere."

"Mmm." She glanced at him sharply, then looked away.

"What?"

"Nothing." She patted a Tupperware container. "I made some cookies earlier. Tell your brother I'll be back later." She removed her apron, hanging it on the peg inside the pantry door.

"Where are you going?"

"Trinity Lakes."

"I can drive you if you like. Whereabouts?"

"I don't want to interrupt you."

"Yeah, I'm hardly busy here, Mom."

"I'm sure your brother would appreciate a hand around the place."

"Not from me he wouldn't." When it came to ranch work, Jackson had been pretty blunt in his assessment of Cooper's efforts and skills in the past. He'd rather pay someone to get it done right than have Cooper mess things up. Apart from when it came to finances and bookkeeping and all the website things. "Come on, Mom. I'll take you to the diner. Or the Bellbird Café."

"Now they do make a nice scone," she said wistfully.

"Okay then. It's a date. You want to leave now?"

"Give me five minutes."

"See you in the car."

She nodded, and he wondered where in Trinity Lakes she was planning on going. And why she'd looked at him like that before. Almost like she recognized the cat. Which was stupid. Besides, didn't all cats look the same?

Thirty minutes later they were sitting in the Bellbird Café. Mom had a silver teapot which was emitting a pretty funky aroma while he sipped the best cappuccino he'd had in months. Between them they had a two-tiered platter of delicacies he figured was probably way too calorie-laden, but that his mom deserved. Besides, what was a son to do when his mom walked into the joint and smiled? Her pleasure had started the moment he opened the door for her, when a tinkling sound rang out, that the owners later said replicated the bellbird of the east coast of Australia. The café's walls were yellow, with mismatched porcelain plates of antique design, which matched —or didn't—the teacups and saucers other patrons were using. A glass cabinet held an assortment of pastries and things he had never seen before, and he guessed his mom hadn't either, so it was only right that a loving son ignore her protests and get the lot.

The owner smiled and plated up the pastries all fancy. "Enjoy your afternoon tea."

Hey, it was still morning, but whatever. This could count as lunch.

And the food was delicious—he was a big fan of this chocolate and coconut-dusted cake square called a lamington—and it was nice to spend time with his mom in this way. He studied her as she talked about the Bible study group she attended with Lynette Franklin and Lil Ladan and some others. Her gray-streaked hair looked so much more stylish than a few years ago, and her blue eyes sparkled as she shared. His heart eased. It was so nice to see her looking happier these days. To spend time with her like this, especially when he had lived away for the best part of a decade, studying then working in California, felt special. Like something he should do more often.

They couldn't finish all the food, so he asked for it to be

packed to-go—"You can enjoy it later, Mom"—and accompanied her to the nearby Village Shoppes Emporium in Cohen's old hardware site. The building had been converted a few years ago into indoor markets with the floor space transformed into a series of cubbyhole-type stalls. The space was decorated like an old western town, with murals and painted props suggesting an old church, a barbershop, a school, and more. Each stall had different products to sell: candles, handcrafted toys, vintage books, jewelry, furniture, recycled fashion, and while some had store-owners manning their booths, customers could also purchase items from a centralized counter.

"I love this place," Mom said.

Yeah, it wasn't exactly his scene, but he figured tourists probably enjoyed it.

"And I thought it would be the perfect place to get a present for Lexi's birthday."

"Is it soon?"

"On Sunday."

Mr. Johnson at the counter offered them both complimentary honey-sticks, and while Mom refused, he accepted. He might have millions in the bank but free was free, right?

He glanced at the nearby leather-goods stall—he bet Jackson would love those big fancy buckles—while Mom dithered over scarves with vintage appeal.

"Which do you think she'd like better?" she asked, holding up a green-and-cream one, and one more brightly patterned in pinks, yellows and reds.

"I'm no fashion expert, Mom."

"They're all so pretty." She touched a blue and peach one, smiling wistfully. "But which do you think she would like best?"

He shrugged. "She's got the sunny personality of that one," he said, pointing to the pink one, "but I've seen her wearing more green so maybe that one."

"That's what I wondered too."

"I can buy the other, and say I was inspired by you."

Mom smiled, and he was again taken by surprise at how much younger that made her look. It might sound weird, but his mom was pretty. He wondered if she'd ever fall for someone again.

As they paid for their loot—in addition to the scarves Mom found a vintage teacup and saucer set she figured would suit Lexi's retro vibe—he noticed Mr. Johnson at the counter talk to Mom. He stepped back, watching as the two of them talked. Mom flicked back her hair, and he swallowed a smile. Really? Was Jackson or Ellie aware?

"What was that?" he asked as he stowed their packages in the car.

"What was what?" she asked.

"You and Mr. Johnson." He opened her door. "He looked like he was flirting with you."

"Me? Don't be silly."

He smiled and gently closed her door. Looked like another family meeting was gonna have to happen soon. It was weird. His mom had been single for nearly all his life. For her to find someone new would be different for them all. But she deserved happiness, and he'd seen Mr. Johnson in church and knew him as a good man, always helping out in various ways. He was pretty sure he'd heard Mr. Johnson mentioned by Ellie as a volunteer at the historical museum.

He pressed the ignition, glanced at her. "It's okay if you find someone, Mom."

"I'm too old," she protested. "Besides, your father—"

"Is dead." That's what he'd been legally declared. And Donald Reilly had been dead to them for the seven years prior to the court's ruling.

"But there was never a burial."

"He's gone, Mom. You don't need to feel guilty or whatever it is. You're allowed to find someone else again."

Her head bowed, and she fingered the blue and peach scarf he'd bought her. "I never thought I could."

He held her hand. "Mom, you deserve to find happiness. I think the others would agree that you've worked so hard for us that it's your time to slow down and enjoy life a little more."

She shook her head. "It seems so decadent to be a woman who even considers taking time to do that. Besides, what man would want to consider an old worn-out creature like me?"

"Mom, don't say that about yourself." He squeezed her hand. "You're beautiful. And people have seen how hard-working and caring you are. And now with the ranch doing better, and Jackson and Lexi living there, you can afford to think of yourself a little more."

She sighed. "I can't believe we're even having this conversation."

Truth be told neither could he. But it seemed it was something that had to be said. "Mom, I love you. We all do. And we want you to be happy. And if that means you take the occasional day off to go do something fun with friends—and no, I don't just mean Bible study with Lynette and Lil—then you should do it."

Her chuckle was raspy. "It's funny to hear the workaholic talking about taking time off."

He shrugged. "I guess I've learned a few things recently about the importance of balancing work with play."

She nodded. "It is easy to get caught in life's ruts and forget to make the most of life while we can."

"So, where are we going now? Have you got somewhere else you'd like to see?"

"One more stop."

"The grocery store?" he guessed.

"No. Turn onto Wainscott Drive."

Huh. Did Mom have a meeting at the Country Club? Maybe

she was taking his 'play' advice more seriously than he'd thought.

But when she tapped his shoulder and directed he take the next right, his heart tensed. Surely not. What would Mom need here?

His mouth dried as she instructed him to pull up outside the Martins' house, where the sounds of dogs barking came from the vet clinic on the left. "What are we doing here, Mom?"

She smiled at him. "You'll see."

Uh oh. He had a feeling she was taking his advice a step way too far.

CHAPTER FIVE

The caterwauling from half a dozen dogs made it near impossible to hear. Thank goodness Nick was at work and not at home trying to catch up on sleep with all this racket. "What did you say?" Jess shouted into the phone.

"We've decided to stay another two weeks," her dad replied.

They had? She glanced at the yappy cocker spaniel that needed its glands expressed. A super fun part of the job.

The door chime sounded. Great. Last she'd checked, the waiting area was already full, and her appointments were already running late. "I gotta go, Dad. Have fun. Say hi to Mom for me."

"Love you, sweetie. Thanks for understanding."

"Of course! You deserve it. Love you both. Talk later."

She ended the call, her shoulders slumping. Of course her parents should have fun in the sun while they could. But knowing they'd be absent for another three weeks instead of one felt incredibly long. How had Dad ever managed to run this practice on his own for so many years? She was barely keeping her head above water let alone making any headway. Even just to have Mom back on reception would help so much. She was drowning, and the sense of overwhelm felt very real.

Blinking back a rush of tears, she focused on poor Dolly, got her sorted, then clipped her nails, something her owner, Mrs. Jansson always feared to do, having caused poor Dolly's infection after a too-vigorous clipping two years ago.

She stroked Dolly's golden hair, then helped her from the steel exam table. Braced her shoulders. If memory served correctly, she had to give an antihistamine injection to Hallie Hollaway's cat, Bandit, then neuter the Petrowksi's rabbit, then deal with the bull mastiff making aggressive barking noises. She could do this. "God, give me strength," she muttered. But it felt like she'd need to try harder to make sure the mask didn't slip.

She opened the door, and the noise in the waiting room hit her like a hurricane. Her thumping headache instantly ratcheted up several knots. She pasted on a smile. "Here you go, Mrs. Jansson. Dolly should be good as gold now."

"Oh, sweetheart." Mrs. Jansson cradled the dog to her chest.

She permitted herself a moment to enjoy the sight of reunited pooch and owner, before the noise ate into her awareness again. "We can fix that up now if you like."

"Oh, but I didn't bring my check book. Can I put it on account?"

Jess blinked. Then remembered that Dolly's owner had used this tactic before. What had Dad done? Was this the one who always quibbled over prices?

"Your father always let me," the older woman wheedled.

He did? Jess pushed up from her haunches and moved to check the accounts on the computer, as the bull mastiff snarled at the little girl holding the bunny. Oh, if only she had an assistant to help her. *Lord, please help!*

"Get your dog away from my daughter," snapped Mrs. Petrowski.

"I'd be able to if she didn't hold it out like food for Captain here," the dog owner growled back.

That thing about pet owners looking like their pets? Totally true. She'd dealt with Captain before, and often thought the dog's snarly nature would be better named with the addition of a Crunch.

Hallie sidled up to her. She, at least, had her cat contained in a plastic carrier. "It looks like you're really busy. I can come back later, if you prefer."

But "later" was not guaranteed to be any quieter. "If you're happy to wait, you'll be next. But thank you." She glanced back at Mrs. Jansson. "It looks like you still have an amount outstanding from the last visit—"

"That can't be right. I always pay on time."

Argue, or leave it for Dad to sort out on his return? He'd better enjoy his vacation. "You can take that up with my parents on their return. Today's charge is still to be paid."

"But I told you, I left my check book behind."

And asking some members of the older generation to figure out online payments was a battle she had no time or energy to deal with now. Jess glanced at the others in the waiting room, all of whom seemed way too interested in this battle over payment. Was that because they thought whatever she would say next was a precedent for their own cases? She dragged in a breath. "Then you'll have to leave Dolly here until you return with your check book."

"What? Are you holding poor Dolly to ransom?"

She was sorely tempted to hiss at the woman to keep her voice down. "I'm simply looking after her until the services performed have been paid for." Another glance at the others revealed a mix of approval and horror. "I'm sorry, but this is a business, and my time is valuable, and—"

"Are you saying my time isn't?"

She couldn't do this anymore. "I'm sorry Mrs. Jansson, but

surely you can see I am far too busy to keep arguing. You'll need to take this up with my father." She moved around the counter and drew Dolly from her owner's arms. "I'll make sure Dolly is safe until you return with your check book."

Dolly started squirming, yelping in protest, just like her owner.

Jess felt like a heel, but if she gave in now, then every man and his dog would try it on. She moved to the back room and placed Dolly in the playpen, giving her a rawhide treat. She returned, ignoring Mrs. Jansson's loud complaints as she glanced at the list of appointments.

"Now, Hallie, I know your cat was next, but I'm going to have to take Captain," so the noise would be halved, "so I hope you don't mind waiting a few moments more."

"That's fine," Hallie said softly, her eyes holding sympathy.

"Well, I mind." Mrs. Petrowski frowned. "Why should he get to go first simply because his dog is so ill-mannered?"

Jess ignored that, mouthed a "thank you" to Hallie who smiled and talked to little Veronica Petrowski about bunnies, and gestured to the exam room.

She was closing the door when the chime announced someone else had entered. "Won't be long," she called.

How she hoped Mrs. Jansson would simply do the right thing and return to pay like she was supposed to. Martin's Veterinary Services didn't need more drama.

Thankfully, Captain was a simple yearly kennel cough injection—something the tattooed owner refused to watch—and if she juggled scheduled appointments she could probably deal with the shorter ones first and help clear the line. Sure enough, five minutes later she was back, fixing up Captain's payment— apparently scare tactics worked, as his owner didn't want to see his beloved dog detained and didn't quibble over the cost—and after fixing him up, she looked across to see two new faces were now sitting in the waiting area.

Her eyes widened. What was Cooper doing here—with his mom? "C-can I help you?"

"I think we can help you," Beth Reilly said, standing.

"What?"

Before Jess knew what was happening, Mrs. Reilly had excused herself to the others and hustled Jess and Cooper into the exam room.

"I'm sorry, Mrs. Reilly, but what's going on? I have animals to see, and I'm already behind schedule, and—"

"You need an assistant, right?"

"Well, yes. But Dad's away, and he called this morning to say they're extending their vacation, and—"

"Cooper can help you," Beth stated.

Cooper frowned. "What?"

"No."

"No, Mom."

"Oh, go on," Beth patted his shoulder. "Consider it your good deed of the day."

Good deed? She might be overworked, but she wasn't that desperate. "Thank you for trying to help, Mrs. Reilly, but I really don't think this would work," Jess said firmly.

"Why not? Cooper designed the scheduling system, didn't he?" Beth turned to him. "You did, right?"

"Well, yeah, but—"

"And now you don't have a job…"

"You don't?" Jess frowned at him. Why not?

"I, um, I'm looking for a new one."

Oh. She'd thought he loved his job. "I can't afford to train someone."

"And he doesn't need to be trained, does he?" Beth Reilly continued. "He designed the system you use here. And he loves animals too, don't you, son?"

"Yes, but Mom, she doesn't want my help—"

"But she *needs* your help. You heard Mrs. Jansson as she was leaving." Her gaze held apology as she eyed Jess. "I'm afraid she was muttering all kinds of things about you, and it wasn't at all complimentary."

Jess pressed her lips together. That was no surprise. Trying to be kind often had a way of backfiring on the generous.

Beth elbowed Cooper and he sighed. "Fine then. I'm happy to help if you want me to. But only if you want me to."

Oh, she *really* didn't want him to. But judging from the fresh round of barking from the back room she really didn't have much choice. This beggar couldn't afford to be choosy. Apparently she was that desperate, after all. "I can't pay you."

"Do you know how much he's made in recent years?" Beth grinned. "He doesn't need pay."

"Consider it volunteer work," he mumbled.

The noise in the waiting room swelled again. Then a voice called, "How much longer do we have to wait?"

Dolly started barking, and everything suddenly seemed too much. "Fine. But I still don't have time to train you."

"I'll figure it out," he said.

She rubbed a hand over her face, praying she could keep it together. "Okay. When can you start?"

"Well, I'm sure he can start immediately," Beth said. "You're not doing anything else now, are you, son?"

He sighed, shook his head. "I can start now. But what are you going to do?"

"You'll be a few hours, won't you? I think I'll see if Maria has any time available to do my hair." She glanced at Cooper. "You don't mind if I drive your car do you?"

"Uh, no."

"Oh, and you might need to see if those treats we got before would be suitable for Jess here." She sent Cooper a look complete with raised eyebrows that suggested something significant.

Whatever. She didn't have time for this. "I really have to deal with my next appointment."

"Of course you do. Cooper, give me the keys, and I'll bring in Jess's lunch."

Lunch? As if hearing the word her stomach growled.

"Better get it quick, Mom. That sounded scary."

Reluctant amusement pushed past her frustration. "Th-thank you."

Beth patted Jess's arm. "I was thinking about you earlier today, and remembering how hard it is to do things alone. Don't be a martyr, not when people want to help."

"Yes, ma'am."

Beth smiled, then pointed a finger at Cooper. "Behave."

"Yes, Mom."

What had just happened? Had Cooper's mom turned into her Fairy Godmother? Jess returned to the waiting room, and invited Veronica and her mom and rabbit inside. "Mr. Reilly has offered to take care of the desk."

The phone rang, and she gestured for him to answer it. His lips twitched, and he answered it. "Hello, this is Martin's Veterinary Services. How can we help?"

She gestured for Veronica and company to walk inside, just as she heard Cooper say, "No, this is Cooper, not James. He's away on vacation. Now, how can we help?"

By the time she returned with a freshly diagnosed rabbit—too many carrots had caused an upset stomach—the waiting room held a semblance of the calm she recalled from when her mom helmed the clinic. She dealt with Hallie's cat—poor Bandit would be drowsy and sore for a while, and didn't love his wide plastic collar—then returned to treat a pet hamster and turtle, then gently advised poor Mrs. Clarkson that the reason her dog was not walking too well was because of old age. Sweet-faced Gingernut was probably going to suffer unless medicated, and really, the kindest thing was to consider euthanasia, even though that was an option nobody ever liked to consider.

"But I've had her for fifteen years," Mrs. Clarkson said, with tears in her eyes.

"I know." Jess swallowed her own emotion. "And she's been a wonderful companion, but she's in pain."

"I can't. I just can't."

Her heart wrenched. "I know it's hard, but I'm only saying this because I know you love her so, and don't want to see her suffer."

Mrs. Clarkson shook her head. "I can't do this today."

"And you don't have to. But perhaps consider it soon."

"How much does that cost?"

Oh, the joys of balancing the encouragement of pet ownership with that of dwindling budgets. She knew some people who prioritized feeding their pets over themselves. "We can talk about that next time."

"No, I want to know."

Jess drew out the laminated card that showed the price of such procedures, which drew a hitched breath and then a sigh. "It should get warmer soon, don't you think? I don't need to pay for heating as much."

Oh, poor lady. She'd have to see if Mrs. Clarkson would qualify for one of her father's benevolent cases, where those facing financial or other hardships had their fees waived. "We'll sort things out," she promised. "The main thing is that Gingernut is not in pain."

The older woman was openly crying now. "I don't know how I'll live without my Gingernut."

Moisture coated Jess's eyes. "I'm so sorry." She offered the box of tissues. Mrs. Clarkson took two and blew her nose. "How about I carry Gingernut out to your car?"

Jess gave her time to compose herself then walked her out, holding Gingernut in her arms, shaking her head at Cooper when he raised his brows. She placed the old faithful dog in her travel kennel, made sure it was appropriately strapped in, then hugged Mrs. Clarkson. "I'm available to talk, whenever you need me."

"Thank you."

Jess blew out a breath as she watched Mrs. Clarkson drive away, wondering if it was wise to let the tearful woman drive. She took a moment to compose herself then re-entered the clinic. A glance revealed two more regulars waiting to be seen. "I just need a minute," she muttered to Cooper, before entering the room.

She moved to the sink and splashed her face with water hoping that the cold would alleviate the redness sure to be around her eyes. There was a tap on the door but before she could say "just a moment" the door opened and she turned to see Cooper.

"Hey, is everything—? Aw, Jess." He shut the door behind him. "What's wrong?"

"I'm fine," she said, pivoting away so he couldn't see her chin wobbling.

"No, you're not. What's happened?"

It took a moment before she could speak. "I just hate telling a woman that her pet is going to die. You think I'd be better at this by now. Mrs. Clarkson is such a sweet lady, and is struggling financially, and when she's tossing up whether she can afford to put her beloved pet out of its misery or pay for heating it sometimes gets to me, okay?"

"Oh, Jess."

His sympathy crawled under her defenses and she had to hold her breath to keep from turning and spilling all her emotions in front of him. She was tougher than this. Had to be tougher than this. How else was she going to get through the rest of her day?

"So we're not charging her." He said this as a statement, not a question.

She shook her head. "I'm pretty sure she qualifies for Dad's special discretionary fund for charitable causes."

"You've always had a kind heart."

His words spurted more emotion, and she had to surreptitiously wipe away yet more tears.

"When have you last eaten?"

"I don't know." She glanced at the wall clock. "Breakfast?"

"Then you're well overdue for a break."

"But—"

"No buts. I'll keep them at bay."

"Thank you."

He smiled, and her heart contracted a little. "There's a little something on the kitchen counter that Mom thought you might like."

"What is it?"

"Go see." He pointed to the door that led through to the back, thus avoiding those still waiting. "Go that way. I'll deal with anyone who dares to complain."

She nodded, and grabbed her phone, and moved out the back, through the room that held poor Dolly—how long until Mrs. Jansson found her check book?—and through into the house. She switched on the electric kettle, patted Bess and Mary, and visited the bathroom, returning in time to pour just-boiled water over a teabag into her favorite mug. Then noticed a cardboard takeout container decorated in the distinctive pink and gray stripes of the Bellbird café. Was this Mrs. Reilly's surprise?

She opened the box and found heaven, grabbing a lemon and lavender cupcake, and inhaling the delicate aroma, before devouring it in three bites. Oh, God bless Beth. A long apple and cream-filled pastry was next, and she'd just finished that when the door opened and Cooper appeared.

"Are you feeling better?"

"These are so good," she mumbled, as pastry flecks escaped her.

He grinned. "I took Mom there earlier and I'm pretty sure she's now in love with the Bellbird's chef."

"Me too," she mumbled.

His smile faded.

"I mean, these are really good."

He nodded. "Well, take your time. It's all good out there, I told them you needed a potty break."

"You what?"

He shrugged. "It was the language they understood, given the small kids. And it was true, right?"

Her cheeks grew hot, and she focused on drinking her tea.

He pointed to the fruit bowl which held a hand of bananas. "You might want to make sure you eat something that won't just be a sugar high."

"Yes, Doctor Reilly."

"You're welcome, Doctor Martin." His smile flashed, then he closed the door.

Honestly. What was with the man? One minute he was behaving like he didn't want to be here, the next he was acting like a concerned boyfriend. She didn't understand the man at all. But she did appreciate his thoughtfulness and his willingness to help today. She owed him. Big time.

By the time she'd finished her tea and eaten her apple—she wasn't going to meekly agree to all his suggestions today—she felt much better. A quick swipe of makeup covered most of the ravages of her emotions from before. She entered the clinic's waiting area only to see Mrs. Jansson arguing with Cooper at the desk as she waved her check book.

"But the records show you still owe for the previous two procedures as well."

"But she said to talk to her father," Mrs. Jansson said.

"By 'she' are you referring to Dr. Jessica Martin?"

"You know I am, young man. Although why I am talking to you when I should be talking to her I don't know." She turned, spotted Jess. "There you are! Would you tell this young man that you said I did not need to pay for my other procedures?"

Jess's shoulders sagged. "I said you needed to pay for today, then Dolly would be released back into your care. And you will still need to pay for the other procedures."

Mrs. Jansson gasped. "I can't believe you are so cruel! I have a mind to refer you to the sheriff. Surely it cannot be legal to hold a dog captive in exchange for money. That smacks of kidnapping if you ask me."

"It's called business, Mrs. Jansson," Cooper said calmly. "And I think you'll find the law agrees. In fact, maybe you could do us a favor and speak to the police and we could invite them to come here. Then they could explain to you that someone who doesn't pay the bills they owe is basically a thief."

She gasped. "How dare you?"

"How dare I speak the truth? You know the simplest method would be for you to pay what is owed."

She clenched her hands, then snatched a promotional pen from the cup and hissed "How much do I owe?"

He read the numbers from the computer screen and she scribbled out two more checks, flinging them at him with all the flair and grace of a star from *Days of Our Lives*.

She turned to Jessica. "I am never coming here again. You people are money-grubbing parasites—"

"Mrs. Jansson, I am sorry you feel—"

"Where is my Dolly? I demand to see Dolly immediately!"

"I'll go get her now," Jess soothed. "Please wait here."

She went to the back, leashed Dolly and handed her to Mrs. Jansson who snatched the lead. "I should've known what you are like. Getting your boyfriend to do your dirty work—"

Jess's mouth sagged.

"—and pretending to care about us when really you only care about the money!"

"Now that's enough." Cooper's voice held a tightness she'd never heard before. "Dr. Martin is one of the most hardworking people I've ever come across, and one of the most compassionate. How dare you malign her character like that?"

"You would say that, seeing as you're her boyfriend, after all."

"I am not."

His words shafted her heart.

"And your actions today, in front of witnesses," he gestured to those still waiting for their appointments, their eyes widened in horrified fascination, "only show the quality of your character, not Dr. Martin's. Please leave."

"But—"

"Goodbye. We're sorry our services have not met with satisfaction. We trust the next veterinarian you find will meet your requirements."

Mrs. Jansson stuck her nose in the air and exited, and one of the local farmers clapped his hands.

"The only vet who will meet that stingy piece of work's requirements will be one who doesn't charge a dime." He nodded to Jess. "Never you mind her, Doc. She's always been tighter than a fish's behind, excuse my French."

Jess nodded, her lips pressed together, as she vacillated between choosing to laugh or cry. She settled for a long sigh instead, thanked the farmer, then spoke to the young Jeffries family. "Now, what's this about a new puppy needing his first vaccinations?"

———

SHE WORKED TOO HARD. Anyone could see that. Here she was, past five at night, and she was still treating pets and their owners while fielding phone calls. The scheduling system he'd set up two years ago was synchronized with both her cell and an automated booking system, and already tomorrow's appointments were backed up. And when the unexpected happened, as in the case of a run over dog that needed emergency surgery, the appointments backed up further.

Yet the nature of her work—the nature of Jessica herself—meant she couldn't turn anyone away. She cared too much, which saw her absorb the shock and emotions of fraught pet owners, blaming herself when she didn't meet her own high standards. It was just as he'd suspected last May, that she was running close to burnout. He didn't know how she'd managed this past week without her parents to help bear the load of appointments and administration. He now understood his mom's manipulations—why she'd tricked him in order to get him to help. He couldn't blame her. Part of him even appreciated it. For he guessed few people knew just how burdensome this job was, and how stressed Jess was. Even if Jess seemed to be in denial herself.

He remembered reading an article last year, one that had scared him enough to speak out. Veterinarians had among the highest suicide rates of all professions. And after working here just one day—more like only half a day—he could understand why. Too many animals to be seen. Too many emotions to balance. Too often on the receiving end of people's anxiety. No wonder Jess was stressed. He felt stressed just trying to figure out how to help her slow down, and he was pretty sure she was embarrassed about him seeing her cry earlier today.

She shouldn't have worried. Her tender-heartedness only increased his admiration, and had drawn fresh resolve to help however he could. Starting with ensuring Mrs. Clarkson's debts were paid, and injecting a fresh sum into the vet clinic's charitable account.

The last patient left, and she locked the door and swung the sign to closed, and sighed. "What a day."

"Is it always like this?"

Her lips twisted. "Would you believe me if I said this was a quiet day?"

"Quiet?"

She rubbed her eyes. "No farm and ranch visits so no large animals to deal with."

He glanced at the screen. "Do you have them tomorrow?"

She covered her mouth as she yawned. "I try to schedule it so Mondays, Wednesdays and Fridays are for household pets in town, and on Tuesdays and Thursdays I do the larger animals and farms."

"And every Saturday you work a half day."

"Half day, whole day, it's much the same these days."

"You work too hard."

"Says the workaholic."

"Yeah, as someone who has skated pretty close to burnout I recognize the signs. Jess," he softened his voice, "you need to take some time for you."

"I do."

"How?"

"I go out."

"I don't mean church."

She glanced at him quickly, her expression saying his words hit home.

"Look, I'm worried about you."

"You don't need to be. I'm not your responsibility."

No. And while she might've said she'd forgiven him, it looked like it would take time to get back to feeling like things were normal between them.

She sighed. "Thank you for your help today. It really made a difference."

"I'm glad." Bless Mom for thinking of it. "But I think you need to work on your scheduling system."

"What's wrong with it?" Defensiveness loaded her words.

"You keep saying yes, Jess. You get texts on your phone and keep adding more to the schedule, and you literally don't have enough hours in the day to fit in all the things you try to do. You need to be kind to yourself, let yourself be human and practice some self-care occasionally."

"Self-care?" Her nose wrinkled. "Like taking long baths?"

He didn't want to imagine that. Well, he did, but he knew he shouldn't. He blew out a silent breath. "Something like that."

"But I can't let animals suffer."

"I know." He studied her, then she bent her gaze away.

His heart grew sore. What could he say to help her?

"I can help again tomorrow."

She rubbed her chin. "Thank you, but I won't need help then."

"Because you're out visiting farms?" She nodded. "Then I'll come back Friday."

"You really don't need to do that."

"But I want to."

"Why?"

"Because I care about you. And it's what friends do."

"Friends." She eyed him, lips rolled in, and he felt himself being weighed. Then she sighed. "I thought you were looking for a new job."

"I am."

She arched a brow.

"Look, if you don't want me to work here, I don't need to."

She ducked her head. "I don't mind."

Yes. He'd take that as a win. "If you don't mind me working for you, then let me help you tomorrow. Unless you really don't want to let me."

"Not let you? The only reason I'm saying no is because there is literally nothing you can do."

"I could drive you places. Get out the instruments you need."

"You know the difference between mosquito forceps and doyen forceps, do you?"

He'd Google it. "Yep."

"Go on then. What is it?"

Why'd she have to call his bluff? "One is, ah, a tool for checking a mosquito"—he internally rolled his eyes at himself. Who cared about mosquitoes?—"and the other is for a donkey's teeth?"

Her lips flicked up. "Nice try, but no."

"What is it then, Doc?"

"Mosquito forceps are used in microsurgeries, like skin biopsies and holding blood vessels, while doyen forceps are used to grip internal organs and secure bleeding during surgical procedures."

"Gross."

"See? That's why you would be useless as my assistant. If you can't stomach that, then how are you going to cope with a cow's stillbirth?"

Hmm. Maybe she had a point. "You're pretty tough."

"I like to think so."

"But you still need to do things to relax."

"I do."

"Yeah? What?"

She shrugged. "I'm meeting a friend for dinner on Friday."

"Nice." He didn't ask who. That would be nosy. But he really hoped it wasn't the firefighter dude.

She eyed him, chewing her lip.

"What is it?"

"Why did you quit your job?"

He winced. Should he tell her? Why not? "It was more a forced restructure."

Her eyes widened. "Ouch."

"Yeah. I really thought they valued me more than they did, but when I saw the severance check I decided I didn't need to feel too loyal. They obviously were willing to pay to get me out of there."

"I'm sorry."

He shrugged. "Stuff happens. But I'm almost glad in a way."

"What way?"

"It got me out of the rut of thinking that work would always have to be this way. I know I work hard, but I realize now that I need to leave some room to relax."

She nodded. "I heard something similar recently."

So had he. But where?

She yawned again.

"Hey, I should scram, let you have dinner." He was tempted to ask if she'd want to have dinner with him, but refrained. It had been a big day, and he didn't want to push things too far on the first day of what he hoped would lead to reconciliation. But if Next Door Nick was her Friday night date maybe he should. No way was some new dude going to steal his girl from under his nose. "On second th—"

"Thanks again."

Right. That sounded like a no to dinner, then. He kept his invitation—his hopes—in his back pocket. "See you Friday, then."

"I do really appreciate your help."

"Any time." He headed to the door.

"How are you getting home?"

"I messaged Mom earlier. She's back home now, and said Lexi can pick me up after her shift at the hospital."

"Tell them I said hi. And tell your mom thanks."

"Will do." He was tempted to linger, but settled for, "Goodnight."

CHAPTER SIX

ow was your day?

Jess stared at BizC's message, wondering how to respond. She'd taken Cooper's advice and practiced a little self-care. She'd just finished taking a bath complete with nectarine bath bomb, and even read a book surrounded by peach-scented candles, while drinking a fancy herbal tisane, all supplied by Trinity Lakes Organics store. Strangely enough, it had helped her relax, even if the concept of sitting in now-dirtied water felt a tad ridiculous to her scientific mind. And now, having wrinkled to appropriate prune consistency, then applied peach-and-vanilla scented moisturizer, she'd just finished painting her toenails, and thought she'd done a pretty good job.

The phone buzzed again with its reminder she needed to respond. So how should she reply? With the truth. *Good. Bad. And everything in between.*

BizC: *Are you okay?*

For some reason that made her think of Cooper and his checking in on her several times today. She had teetered between appreciation for his concern and resentment for his intrusion into her life. What kind of guy dumped a girl then basically barged straight back into it? Although, to be fair, his barging back in was more his mother's doing than his own. Though clearly he was up to the task his mother thought he was capable of.

I'm okay now, she typed. *Glad to be talking to you.*

Here is something funny I came across a while ago. Hope it makes you smile.

She clicked on the link. A graphic with a chalkboard popped up. "My teacher said don't worry about spelling. In the future there will always be autocorrect. I'm eternally grapefruit."

She chuckled. Typed back: *That is funny.*

See, I knew you had an excellent sense of humor.

Because it matches yours?

Exactly.

She did laugh out loud at that. *Thanks for making today better.*

Any time.

Her heart caught. Had Cooper meant it when he'd said the same to her earlier? Did he really mean that he would help her any time she needed him? It had taken her off guard, but it *was* a kind, no, a super generous offer.

She sighed, regretting her snippy behavior. She might have forgiven him, but she obviously had a long way to go in the graciousness department. He'd been so helpful today, fielding calls, dealing with angry Mrs. Jansson effectively. He'd taken the heat for her, allowing her to focus on what she needed to do, and proved his thoughtfulness time and again.

She could now see why her parents had made such a good team over the years, with her mother's compassion allowing her to connect with the pet owners and freeing her dad to use his skills. And yet, Cooper Reilly had to be the most overqualified administrative assistant in history. A man with post doctorate qualifications from MIT working as her secretary?

And what had he meant about losing his job? Anyone who let him go was incredibly foolish and short-sighted. His departure would be their loss, and no doubt, his gain. It would certainly only be a matter of time before he found a better job somewhere. Probably in New York, or Tokyo or London, or someplace where they valued people with his kind of skills. The thought of someone with his kind of skills answering the phone at the vet clinic made her smile. The thought of him moving to New York or overseas made her smile fall away.

BizC's message popped up again. *So, have you got another photo, or do I have to imagine you as a cat?*

You want a photo of me? she asked.

Yes!

Okay, he could have a photo. She stretched out her foot, admiring her handiwork, then took a photo that she uploaded and shared. Then waited, waited, waited…

BizC: *Ha ha ha. You're funny. How did you know I have a foot fetish?*

What?

BizC: *Jokes. But seriously, there are some creepy dudes out there. Don't go sending that pic to just anyone.*

Embarrassment wrapped around her as much as if she'd sent an accidental bikini shot to the pastor. She closed down the screen. She didn't know what to say. Then opened it again. Could she get the photo back?

One of the handy dandy features of this app: yes, she could.

She pressed Unsend on her photo, stuck it in the trash, and immediately closed the app again. But not before she glimpsed his latest message. *Hey, are you still there?*

Her heart was tight. Nope. She wasn't. Clearly trying to connect online like this had been a bad idea.

THURSDAY PASSED AS MOST DID, with the visits to nearby ranches and farms taking her on the road in Big Red. This focus on larger animals saw her called to everything from supervising difficult or first-time cow births, to dealing with horses with gastric ulcers, or being the qualified vet signing off on in-vitro fertilization. The jobs varied widely from the usual domestic animals that she saw, and the chance to drive Big Red and get out to explore more of the beautiful Trinity Lakes area always eased her heart, and made her feel like she had a chance to breathe.

Friday, the weight of numerous appointments awaiting her drew heaviness on her soul. How was she supposed to manage? Except, when a knock on the door revealed Cooper's face, she felt her heart skip a few beats.

"You came."

"You seem surprised. I said I would."

Already she could see the first client of the day exiting their vehicle. She sighed. "Quick, you better come inside."

She was tempted to lock the door behind them but knew Mr. Herman would get cold waiting outside so she left it unlocked.

"Anything I need to know for today, boss?" Cooper asked.

"I'm not your boss."

He shrugged. "Right now I don't have any other, and I'm here ready to work for you, which means you kind of are. And I bet there's a secret part of you that really enjoys telling me what to do and where to go. Am I right?"

He knew her well. She bit back a smile, relief filling her as Mr. Herman entered the space. "Just do what you did the other day," she murmured, before saying in a louder voice, "Hello, Mr. Herman. We'll be right with you. It's not even nine o'clock and yet here you are already."

"I saw this young man enter and figured I might as well too."

Okay, then.

Cooper shot her an apologetic look complete with mouthed "sorry" then invited Mr. Herman to take a seat "While Doctor Martin gets prepared for the day."

"Yes, but I also have a very full day," Mr. Herman complained. "I need to get Cricket fixed up then I'm meeting some people at the Country Club."

"That sounds interesting, but Doctor Martin has a very full schedule too. And considering the clinic is not even technically open yet, let alone it being your scheduled appointment time, I'm sure you can understand that she needs a few more minutes in order to prepare. Now, please take a seat."

That was thoughtful of Cooper. And she noticed his consideration several more times during the day. Fielding phone calls, soothing tempers about costs—did they not know that given the years of training with the associated cost she was actually severely underpaid?—then helping poor Mrs. Clarkson bring in her beloved dog.

Cooper glanced at Jess and her heart broke a little. Poor lady. She knew what she was going to say before the old lady spoke a word.

"Can you please allow some extra time for this?" she asked him in a quiet voice.

"Sure." He made a praying hands gesture, and her heart clenched a little. She might be a professional, but she needed prayer, and Mrs. Clarkson certainly would. She led her to the second exam room, which would allow greater privacy for what would take place.

And the process was as hard as she expected, with Gingernut looking up with pain-filled eyes at her mistress, who could barely see given her own eyes were so wet. Jess talked her through the procedure, assured her that Gingernut would feel no pain, and she prayed for the woman as the dog whimpered one last time then closed her eyes and stilled.

Her own throat closed, and she wiped away tears. Oh, she *hated* this part of the job. And yet, pets didn't live forever, and an end-of-life situation like this had to be better than being hit by a car or dying in pain from snake bite. And while she'd witnessed dozens of similar situations, this one hit hard, and she grieved with Mrs. Clarkson.

Mrs. Clarkson cuddled her pet, then slowly released, forcing Jess to hastily wipe away the wetness on her face, as she handed the older woman a box of tissues.

Mrs. Clarkson blew her nose, her gaze not leaving Gingernut. "She looks so peaceful."

"She is at peace now. No more pain. No more suffering. You did what was best for her."

"I love her."

Jess blinked back more tears. "I know."

Mrs. Clarkson released a shaky breath. "What happens now?"

"That depends on what you need. Would you like us to look after Gingernut here, or would you like her buried in your garden, or have her ashes with you?"

They had a small refrigerated area used for such things, although they encouraged owners to keep their pets near. And yet Mrs. Clarkson was alone in the world, a widow, without children, although she suspected her neighbors might help her out sometimes. Jess knew that her own father had sometimes gone above and beyond and even helped some people dig graves for their pets. She didn't think she had enough physical strength to do that in the rocky ground around here. Then wondered whether Cooper meant what he'd said about helping her anytime…

Mrs. Clarkson wiped away more tears. "I can't believe I never thought about this. Ronnie was sick for so long that we had plenty of time to discuss what he wanted, but poor Gingernut…"

Jess gently rubbed her back as Mrs. Clarkson finally acknowledged that she would like to have Gingernut buried. Again the question of how to help her do that flitted through her mind. Ask Cooper? Just how willing was he to help her out?

"I'll give you a few more minutes to say goodbye," she said, then escaped out to the back passage.

She savored the moment alone, to collect herself and paste on professionalism again. But she could hear Mrs. Clarkson's gentle weeping, which triggered fresh emotion which spilled down her cheeks.

"You're here."

She stilled. And so was Cooper. She couldn't turn around. "Why—?"

"I heard Mrs. Clarkson crying, and went to check on her, then realized you had to be here."

She nodded, pressing her lips together to hold back emotion.

She heard him step closer, the hairs on her arms prickling as if sensing his nearness in the dim light of the hall. She glanced up, met his concerned expression, which only sparked fresh tears she desperately tried to blink away.

"Oh, Jess." His arms opened as if to hug her—something she suddenly, desperately wanted—and then dropped, instead, patting her awkwardly on the shoulder.

Ouch. But okay. She'd totally misread that.

"What can I do?"

She pivoted away again, wiped her face, and drew in a shaky breath. "She wants the dog buried in her garden, but I don't know who to ask to help with that."

"I can do it," he said quietly.

"Would you?"

"I wouldn't offer otherwise. And you know I'm happy to help you any way I can."

She was tempted to ask why again, but figured he'd just say the same as last time. Besides, he only wanted to be friends. He probably just felt guilty about how he'd treated her last year. He clearly wasn't interested in anything more, which was why he'd not bothered to hug her. Her heart whimpered a little, and she squeezed out a "Thanks."

"I'd better get back," he said. "Let me know when she's ready and what to do."

She nodded, and stole another precious moment of quiet, before returning to Mrs. Clarkson, explaining what Cooper had offered to do, which met with her gratitude and thanks.

Fortunately, the long appointment time already booked meant there were only a couple of clients left to see, so she released Cooper from manning the front desk to go help Mrs. Clarkson with poor Gingernut.

"It's okay," she murmured to him. "I've managed doing both roles before and I can do it again. You helping her now is more important."

He nodded, lips pursed.

"I do appreciate you doing this. And don't worry about coming back here after. I'll lock up."

"Are you sure?"

"Positive." She bent up her lips. "Thanks again."

A short time later she glimpsed him escorting Mrs. Clarkson back to her car, carrying a large box that held Gingernut. She excused herself to go hug Mrs. Clarkson, and equipped Cooper with what her father usually supplied in such circumstances, and prayed that all would go well.

The remaining appointments were straightforward, and she locked the door, then cleaned up. It was nearly six by the time she returned to the main part of her house, and her stomach gave a growl of protest. Had she eaten lunch today? It was nearly dinner time.

Her thoughts returned to Cooper, and she wondered how he'd gotten on. Bless the man. Burying a dog meant she probably should thank him with something more substantial than mere words. Dinner? But no. That would probably lead him to getting ideas that she wanted to get back together, and while a secret and very foolish part of her might think that a good idea, another part of her knew it wasn't. He'd let her down before.

And she was committed to moving on. Even if BizC had made her second guess herself again.

Her gaze stole to the kitchen, to the freshly rewashed and repainted—

Oh no! She was supposed to be feeding Nick McDavid as her thank you for his help in the fire and cleanup last weekend. How had she forgotten? What could she do at such short notice?

A peek at the fridge revealed nothing magically quick and easy inside. She shut it, sending the takeout menus flapping. Her eyes widened. Okay, so maybe this was overkill, and would probably cost more than her fortnightly food budget, but at least it would be good.

She ordered pasta and salad to-go from Giovanni's then set the table. What time had she told Nick? She'd probably have enough time to have a quick shower before it was delivered. She hoped Nick wouldn't notice the delivery car. And while Giovanni's was a bit fancy, it definitely was good food. And there was a good chance that because Nick was new in town he hadn't had it yet, and would probably enjoy it. Firefighters had to keep their strength up, didn't they?

A niggle of concern pricked. What would Cooper say if he returned? She shooed it away. She'd told him to go home, so he wouldn't return. Besides, even if he did, Jess eating with a man shouldn't bother him. It wasn't like they were together or anything. And it wasn't like she and Nick were doing anything except sharing a meal which was strictly a thank-you dinner. But just to make sure she sent a quick message telling him *thank you* again and that she hoped it had gone well.

As well as can be expected, his reply came not two minutes later.

So she is okay?

She's planning a special memorial garden, and looking forward to spring.

Thanks for your help. I hope you have a good night.

———

A GOOD NIGHT?

After the day she'd had, Jess was the one deserving a good night. What a crazy week. And he'd only caught a glimpse of the pressures she faced on a daily basis. How did she manage to have such stores of compassion for others? Cooper hadn't been kidding earlier. He'd do whatever he could to assist, and he figured Jess deserved a quiet night, good food, good company. He glanced at his phone and smiled. And yeah, if he should be considered good company, all the better.

A short time later he pulled into Wainscott Drive, then parked. The clinic's lights were off, the sign turned to closed, which meant she was done. Good. Hopefully she was feeling relaxed, and hungry, maybe wearing those Goofy sweats like she used to long ago. He exited the car, drew out the items that smelled so good, and walked down the driveway as he'd done dozens of times in the past.

He clutched the flowers, and the pizza box. Thank goodness Lily's Florist was still open, and that Giovanni's did phone orders and good food quick. This was just what a friend did, someone who cared, even if her actions earlier today had made him want more.

Earlier, when he'd seen her red-eyed after dealing with Mrs. Clarkson's dog, everything inside him had ached to hug her, to give comfort. He'd thought he'd glimpsed a vulnerability there, a softness different to her usual stiff stance around him. He'd opened his arms to wrap her in a hug when he'd realized that would make him look unprofessional, and he didn't really want to risk a slapped cheek at the vet clinic. A red handprint mark on a cheek sure would give the gossips like Rhonda Ingalls something to talk about.

So while a hug might be out of the question, he figured the least she deserved was flowers. And Jess had always enjoyed flowers from Lily's Florist. He'd bought a second bouquet for Mrs. Clarkson, who had thanked him for his thoughtfulness when he'd delivered them just now.

He hoped Jess would appreciate the gesture of flowers and food. That she'd feel valued. That she'd know he'd do anything to help her feel secure.

Laughter stole to his ears, and his steps slowed. The back part of Jess's house was lit, and he could see indistinct shapes beyond the window shade. She had company?

A screech from a cat made him clutch the box more closely.

The outside light flickered on. "Who's there?"

Oh. No. He recognized that voice. What was *he* doing here?

He was sorely tempted to ditch the flowers, but instead stepped forward from the shadows. "Just me."

"Who?"

Clearly he was memorable. "Cooper Reilly. I wanted to see Jess."

The he-god frowned, his gaze dipping to the pizza box then trickling back to Jess with something that looked like a smirk.

Cooper's heart tensed. What was she doing with the firefighter dude? Sharing a romantic meal? He bet it wasn't pizza...

Jess appeared, and his breath hitched. Far from looking sad and sorry, she'd dressed up, even if she was wearing jeans and a black top, but she wore makeup, and had styled her hair. "Cooper? What are you doing here?"

Her gaze flicked to his hands, and he was painfully aware of how meager his offerings appeared. "I, er, got these for you."

"Oh, you shouldn't have."

He shrugged, his heart smarting. Yep, he kinda felt that way now as well. Had Super Nick given her flowers too? Probably. It seemed the kind of thing a hero dude would do.

He handed them to her anyway, before he gave into the temptation to throw them away. This was a mistake. She'd moved on. She didn't want him.

Now to make it look like it wasn't nearly the romantic gesture everything screamed it was. "I, um, just wanted to make sure you were okay. I know it was a hard day, and I figured this," he held up the pizza box, "might come in handy for when you need a meal in a hurry."

She bit her lip, and he desperately wanted to explain more. But with the way Nick stood there, all fierce yet amused-looking, like he could see straight past Cooper's lame excuses to the pathetic man inside, he wasn't going to say another thing.

Except, "Good night."

He placed the pizza on the white wrought iron table, and scooted out of there, pretending not to hear her when she called out his name.

Nope. They were done. That ship had embarked on different waters. And he had been left treading water while he wondered where to next.

The drive back to the ranch felt way too long, but at least it allowed time to lick his wounds, to get his act together before facing Jackson, Lexi, and his mom.

"You're back late," Jackson said.

He nodded. "Had to bury a dog."

Lexi and Mom's faces softened, as Jackson said, "At this time of night?"

He shrugged. No way was he going to explain what he'd tried—and failed—to do. "Took longer than I thought."

"That must've been so hard," Lexi said, sympathy in her eyes.

"It was Mrs. Clarkson's dog," he said, glancing at Mom.

She nodded. "Poor lady. She's loved that dog for years. He was her main comfort when her husband died."

"Poor thing." Lexi looked like she might cry. "We should make her a meal."

"She doesn't eat much," he said. He'd wondered that too, but Mrs. Clarkson had said casseroles would be wasted on her.

"So, you're still helping out Jess Martin, huh?" Jackson said, his eyes holding a similar knowing quality to what he'd seen in Nick's earlier.

"She needs help." Especially with her taste in men.

But no. He shouldn't think things like that. Not when he'd proved himself to be anything but reliable. He couldn't blame her for wanting to find someone more suitable.

He reheated leftovers, managed small talk, then when the others settled in to watch a movie, he made his excuses and headed to his room.

He slumped on the bed, drew out his phone, went onto Dream Match.

Still nothing.

Had he embarrassed BlessBess? He was half tempted to paint his own toenails and take a picture and post that to her but didn't think he could explain wanting nail polish very easily to his mom.

He sent BlessBess another message, trying to reconnect, trying to atone.

Was it wrong to be pursuing her, when he couldn't stop thinking about the one who didn't want him? Maybe. Probably.

But if she did reply and they could rekindle the tease and exchange from earlier, then BlessBess would be a great way to put Jess in his rearview mirror.

That was, if she responded.

He read over their exchanges, the jokes, the smiles, the memes, the sharing of personal aspects of their lives. Had his joke about the foot fetish offended her? He could've shared that with Jess and she would've laughed. Well, she would have, until their parting last year. Who knew how she'd respond these days?

His thoughts flicked back to the cozy couple and their cozy meal. His heart rippled, his mouth souring. Maybe it was immature of him to still want what he'd once rejected, but he couldn't help it. Except he'd have to help it. Let her move on, and hope he could do the same.

He glanced back at the last few exchanges with BlessBess. Still nothing. Nada. He'd give it a few more days before giving up. Maybe there was another dream match out there waiting for him. Or maybe God didn't have anybody for him at all.

Meantime, with her parents returning in a few weeks, and doubtless able to help Jess with the veterinary clinic's insane workload, it was probably time to get serious about looking for a job somewhere else. New York, London, Berlin. He didn't care. His range of skills meant he could do work remotely, but more often employers liked him in-house. In fact, he had a resume ready to send to some former clients who'd murmured before about wanting him to work for them.

Before he could think much further, he retrieved his resume from the Cloud, tweaked it, then sent the contact an email, with a subject line that stated "Just in case you're still interested..."

Because right now, he'd be happy to be anywhere far away.

CHAPTER SEVEN

All weekend Cooper's flowers stared at her accusingly.

She should've stopped him and made him listen. She should've explained it was just a thank-you dinner and nothing more. She shouldn't have listened when Nick said to leave him.

But trying to say any of that felt like a conversation too big for a mere text message, and she didn't know what exactly to say in person, so she'd procrastinated until now, when the church service was nearly over, and she figured she could make it clear that she and Nick weren't a thing.

That had become obvious during their meal. While the food was good, the conversation had struggled, apart from a few times when she'd made him laugh as she'd tried to focus on the highlights of her day. Her exchange about a pet hedgehog had been met with his about the hazards of people sleeping in the nude, which had led to some interesting fire rescues over the years. And while neither of them had mentioned names, she still felt like it sailed awfully close to oversharing. And that if telling funny stories about other people were all they had in common, then they could be surface friends without hunting for something deeper which wasn't there.

It hadn't been like that with Cooper. He'd always been quick-witted and kind, yet interested in so many of the same things. They could talk about science and math and research and animals and space and the world and she'd never get bored. They'd never had any of those long stretches of silence that felt edged with boredom like she had with Nick. She bet someone out there would be perfect for him, but it wasn't her. She wanted—needed—someone who knew her, knew what made her tick, knew why she cared for animals. Which sucked for any person new to the area because they'd never really understand what it was about Trinity Lakes that held her heart so. She barely understood it herself. But there was something about the people here, the setting, the community, that brought her heart ease. It was the perfect small town in so many ways, and she liked knowing her roots were firmly established here, which meant she knew who she was, and what her future could be.

Well, she *had*.

Until Cooper had moved away. Then returned. Then kindled deeper levels of affection. Then broke it off. Before returning, repentant, and leaving her wondering what would happen next.

Theo Ladan concluded the sermon and she guiltily bowed her head, her thoughts still tracking separately to the sermon topic, as she prayed for God to have His way.

Later, her phone switched off to avoid any unwanted messages, she met up with Hallie and Jodie during the post-service coffee time. Talking—or rather, listening—to her friends proved a chance to recalibrate her soul, to pretend she was normal, and that her heart wasn't filled with chaotic clutter like it had been earlier.

Then Beth Reilly drew her attention. She was talking to Mr. Johnson from the Village Shoppes Emporium. The indoor market center had been his idea years ago, as a way of showcasing—and occasionally selling—his huge collection of vintage records. Other collectors and craftspeople had joined in, and the stalls were the perfect place to spend hours checking out all that was on offer. If one had the luxury of hours to kill, that was.

Beth and Mr. Johnson seemed to be having quite the cozy time, enough to make Jess wonder if maybe Beth would finally be able to find happiness again. It had certainly been a long time since she'd smiled like that with a man.

A bump on her shoulder drew her attention to Ellie.

"You're back again," Jess said.

"As you can see." Ellie curtsied.

"Seattle can't keep you, huh?"

"We're having a little celebration for Lexi's birthday today, and I have tomorrow off, so I figured it's a great chance to see the fam and my fiancé."

Jasper Cohen smiled across the room from where he was talking to Jackson and Cooper. Cooper shifted, his gaze finding Jess. Her stomach tightened at the drawn expression on his face.

"Hey, you should come."

"To what?" She dragged her attention away from Ellie's brother. He still had the power to magnetize, even after this long.

"To Lexi's birthday lunch at the ranch. Or has Cooper already invited you?"

"No."

"No? What's wrong with him? Well, I know that's an answer that will take half a millennia to answer, so let's just say he should've."

"For *Lexi's* birthday party?"

"It's not a party. Just a gathering. Her parents are coming, and the Cohens and Ladans too, because we're also talking weddings. Jackson is cooking ribs, so it'll be pretty relaxed. Come on. You've been practically part of the family for years."

True. But, "I don't have anything to bring." Apart from half a cold pizza. Had Cooper bought the family size thinking they could share? She shook her head. "And I don't have a present."

"You know Lexi isn't the kind to care about presents. And I *know* she enjoys your presence, so you should come."

Before Jess could protest, Ellie grasped Jess's hand and dragged her to where Lexi was talking with Jackson, which left Jess within a yard of Cooper. She didn't look at him.

"Hey, Lexi, you don't mind that I invited Jess to lunch, do you?"

Couched like that, how could Lexi graciously refuse? Still, Lexi's warm smile held sincerity like her words. "I'd love for you to come. I didn't realize you hadn't been invited."

Jess's heart snagged. Maybe Cooper hadn't said anything because he hadn't wanted her there. She didn't dare look at him in case that was true. Besides, it was too late now.

An hour later she was driving Big Red up the hill, leaving Trinity Lakes as a sparkle of blue behind her. She passed the carefully maintained fence of the Darcy ranch. She'd visited the estate a few times for work, and been overawed at the house and grounds worthy of America's Most Beautiful Homes award. She'd heard it had been built and later renovated to include all kinds of features, like an indoor pool with its own chandelier and kitchen entertaining area, for guests—many of whom were international business clients—to enjoy. She'd been impressed by the stables complex, and the quality and experienced staff which ensured the horses and cattle were cared for in ways that surpassed the care of any non-veterinarians she'd met.

She glanced at the passenger seat, where a little basket was perched, containing hurriedly bought items she figured the Aussie might enjoy. Sure, Lexi could buy her own Vegemite and Milo, but she'd probably enjoy it being given to her. Coupled with a packet of Caramello koalas—the most Aussie thing in the Trinity Lakes grocery store she could find—and she figured it wasn't a bad last-minute gift.

But seeing Cooper again would prove interesting. He'd made zero effort to connect since the Friday night fail of dinner, which made her wonder if he'd even bother to show tomorrow. That, more than anything, was reason to try to talk to him. His presence had made a huge difference at the clinic, so she hoped he'd return. Which probably meant they needed to talk. About that. Nothing else.

Except…

Why had he bought her flowers? Maybe it was just a sweet gesture because he'd seen how upset she'd been. But what if it had been more? Or was that simply some leftover emotion from a year ago, back when she'd thought they'd finally turn their relationship into forever, until he'd made it clear his future was in Silicon Valley, and she was working herself into an early grave?

Her stomach churned. So many things remained unresolved. Life was so different to a year ago, yet in many ways it had stayed the same. But while she might still be overworked, at least she'd made some progress in matters of the heart. Like, she didn't need to apologize for having Nick over for a meal. That was none of Cooper's business, anyway. And if he was upset by that, she didn't want to know what he'd think of her being on Dream Match. Not that she should be bothered by what he thought. She still wasn't sure what to do about Dream Match and BizC. She'd managed to send a quick hi in a message last night, and apologize for her recent silence.

He'd replied instantly. *Good to hear from you. Is everything okay?*

In some ways. But messaging him when she felt conflicted about Cooper felt wrong. But so was leaving him hanging. So she'd figured saying something had to be better than ghosting him. She'd replied with a simple *Yes* she hoped would do the trick. It was an online friendship. It didn't have to mean more.

Just like it was only a real-life friendship with Cooper. Something she doubted would ever mean more.

The grand stone walls of the entrance to the Reilly Ranch drew near. Dermott Reilly's handiwork, which had been an attempt to show his mom his love of landscaping over ranch life, then led to his self-imposed exodus a decade or two ago. He'd moved to the east coast, and joined the Greener Gardens landscaping company in the Independence Islands, and by all accounts was doing really well.

She turned in and parked Big Red next to Cooper's sports convertible. Her heart tightened. The difference between them couldn't be summed up any better. He was all about tech and money and fast-paced city life; she was rusted-on small town, practical, and kept ticking on, even if Big Red had trouble starting every once in a while. It was pointless to think they could make anything work. They were too different. Her heart dropped. Not that it mattered. It was only a matter of time before he'd leave again, anyway.

She clenched her hands on the steering wheel until her knuckles whitened. Then released. Found a smile. This was probably a bad idea, but hopefully there would be enough people as distractions that she needn't get caught up in huge and unnecessary explanations with Cooper. She hoped so, anyway.

Inside, she was welcomed by Beth and Lexi, as the scent of browning meat drifted to them.

"We were going to eat outside but the look of that big gray cloud gave us second thoughts." Lexi shivered. "I'm still adjusting to what winter temperatures feel like after living in Wollongong for nearly ten years."

Jess nodded—she thought that Aussie city was near the beach—and handed over the basket. "Happy birthday."

"Oh, you didn't have to," Lexi said, then glanced up, her eyes sparkling. "But I'm glad you did."

Jess laughed, and was glad to see her gift met with the appropriate level of appreciation. "I figured you'd enjoy some Aussie treats."

"You figured right." Lexi hugged her. "Thank you."

"Come on inside." Beth gestured down the hall. "It's too cold near the door."

Jess removed her boots, placing them near the untidy pile of other shoes near the front door, then joined the others in the living area.

"Look who's here!" Ellie called, getting up from Jasper's lap. "I'm glad you made it."

"I knew where to come. I've been here a few times before," Jess joked.

"It's been a minute since you were last here for a meal," Jackson said, from where he was basting something at the kitchen counter.

The room fell silent, awkwardness stretching between them as people glanced at Cooper, then her, then back again.

"Well, I'm glad you're here now," Lexi said. "Mom, Dad, look what Jess-the-best bought me."

As Lexi showed off her birthday treasures, Jess did her best to smile and pretend everything was alright. But the need to talk to Cooper was growing, to find out if his flowers meant anything more than "sorry you had a bad day."

Maybe she'd been too optimistic in thinking time here at the ranch would make it easier to talk, because there were so many people. Jackson and Lexi, Lexi's parents, Beth, Cooper, Ellie, Jasper and his parents, Pastor Theo and Lil Ladan, and she made thirteen. Cooper had moved to help Jackson outside, but the noise hadn't dimmed. The Cohens, Ladans, Franklins and Ellie and her mom were talking weddings, and Jess enjoyed the chance to listen without the spotlight being on her.

Until Mrs. Cohen turned to her and smiled. "So does this mean you and Cooper are back together?"

Ouch. "Um, no."

"But I understood he is now helping you at the clinic."

"Until he returns to work," she said carefully.

Beth nodded. "He stepped in when there was an overload of patients, didn't he, Jess?"

"Yes."

She caught Beth's mouthed "Sorry."

She shrugged. "Anyway, I don't want to talk about that. I'd much rather hear about this spectacular wedding."

The conversation graciously drifted back to the wedding ceremony, and both the Ladans and Franklins offered thoughts about the service.

"All I know is that I want Mom to walk me down the aisle," Ellie said.

Because she had no father to do so.

"And I want Jess to be one of my bridesmaids."

"Really?"

"Of course! You know I've long thought you were like my sister, even if my brother can't see that."

Her heart panged. It wasn't as a sister that Jess wanted Cooper to see her.

She ducked her head. No, no. She refused to go down that path again. She needed something more than other people's speculations and a bunch of "sorry you're feeling sad" flowers and an almost-hug to build a case on. Besides, what she'd said was true. He wouldn't stay around, and anyway they were too different.

The topic had turned to reception venues, and Jess was soon asked her opinion about the merits of chicken versus steak for mains. She offered her opinion—if they were using Reilly steak, then that was the pinnacle, and most women needed more iron, so that was her pick—and Ellie grew excited about the prospect of a bachelorette high tea.

"Oh, I love a good high tea," Lynette Franklin said. "I

remember we used to have numbers of venues offering them when we lived in Australia."

"Does anyone know if the Bellbird café does them?" Lexi asked.

"They should," Beth Reilly said. "I think the food there is superb."

"That would be fun, wouldn't it?" Jess said to Ellie. "I'd definitely be back for more."

"You went there without me?"

Oh. Awkward. She and Ellie had talked about going for months, but Jess had never found the time. She glanced at Beth.

Beth seemed to recognize her plea as she nodded then turned to Ellie. "Cooper and I visited last week, and he took some of our leftovers to Jess afterwards."

"He did, did he?" Ellie eyed her with a suspicious smile. "You're not together, huh?"

Fortunately, distraction by way of Jackson entering with a tray of meat meant the focus shifted from Jess again. Until she grew aware of those watching her as she watched Cooper enter the room behind him.

She ducked her head, her cheeks hot. It was no good pretending. This meal was making a meal of her, and she'd do well to eat then run. Maybe she'd be saved by someone calling her on her phone—

Her phone! She grabbed it from her bag and switched it on. Then winced.

"What's wrong?" Lexi asked.

"I got a million missed calls. I need to check them."

"Jess, sit down," Ellie instructed. "You need to eat before you do anything, so just relax."

But Mr. Galbraith had called half a dozen times. That didn't mean nothing.

"She's right," Lynette Franklin said. "Take a moment to breathe, eat, refuel your energy before you go out again."

"You know that if you listen to them you'll only start worrying about what you have to do," Cooper said, his eyes on her.

Oh, how well he knew her.

"Besides, the food is ready to eat now," he continued.

"Then we should say grace and start." Jackson smiled at Lexi then glanced at his father-in-law. "Peter, would you say grace?"

Jess closed her eyes as Peter thanked God for His provision, for the blessings of family, friends, and food, and prayed a special birthday blessing on Lexi.

"Amen."

"Thank you." Lexi beamed, as Ellie encouraged her to line up first for the ribs, wings, slaw and salad that had made many a celebratory meal over the years. "But before I do, Jackson and I have a little announcement of our own."

Jackson moved behind her, clasped his hands over her stomach. "We'll have the newest little Reilly joining us in the Fall."

Oh, how special! Jess joined the congratulations as Lexi and Jackson were surrounded with hugs, the movement of people pushing Jess to the side where she bumped into someone. Turned. And faced Cooper.

"Hi," she blurted.

"Hi." His eyes studied her, until movement behind her pushed her closer against him again. "Whoa." He held her upper arms. "Are you okay?"

She nodded, swallowing, as his scent of sandalwood drew memories of moonlit walks and tender hugs. She backed away, but not before she saw his gaze dip to her lips. Her heart thudded. He still cared?

"You know, for two people who say you're not together, you're not doing a great job of convincing us of that," Ellie teased.

Jess twisted away, and joined the line serving food and was relieved to resume her seat, glad when the space next to her was taken by Lil Ladan. She'd eat then run. Lynette was right. Whatever emergency Mr. Galbraith needed her help for she'd face better if she'd just eaten.

So yes, she might've surprised Lil and looked a little greedy with her speed-eating, but she had to leave. For Mr. Galbraith's sake. Not because she was tired of being teased about the unattached Reilly sibling here.

But when she finally moved to the front hall and listened to her messages, she knew it had been a mistake. Mr. Galbraith had a horse exhibiting all the signs of colic. He'd started calling hours ago, while she'd been blissfully shopping, and now she didn't know what would happen. She called him back, wincing at his angry outburst for not picking up three hours ago, before assuring him she was on her way.

"Is everything okay?" Cooper asked.

She shook her head. "Mr. Galbraith is panicking because of Starlight, and I need to leave now."

"I'll come with you."

"No. You should stay."

"I'll come with you," he repeated softly.

"You don't need to—"

"I don't need to stay to hear talk about weddings and babies all afternoon, that's for sure. So I'm coming with you. Surely there'd be something I can do."

She nodded. In cases like this there were always plenty of things people could do. If she needed to do stomach tubing, having an extra pair of steady hands was essential, as owners couldn't always be relied upon to be calm. And judging by Mr. Galbraith's anger, it'd be good to have someone take the heat of his upset so she could concentrate on doing what she could to save his horse.

She made her farewells, apologizing for not staying for cake, while Lexi promised to save some for them. She hurried to Big Red, wondering how Cooper had managed to extricate himself from the situation without too much tease, and checked her supplies. As ever, she'd departed with the veterinarian's equivalent of a doctor's medical bag, with equipment and medications for all kinds of emergencies. And she was prepared for this.

She reversed the truck and was about to leave when Cooper hurried over, holding a thick jacket, a bag, and a cooler. He placed the last in the back then got in, slammed the door. He knew how Big Red rolled. She gunned the truck out the drive, turning left to go up the backroads to the Galbraith farm. It was ten miles away, and the countryside here was bleak and lonely, made even more so with the threatening clouds inching ever closer. And she was stuck here, with the man who'd broken her heart, feeling like she was heading to her doom.

COOPER WAS USED to awkwardness and strained silences—he'd experienced a few such moments in the past two hours—but this felt next level. Why exactly he'd insisted on doing this he didn't really know, except there'd been that moment when Jess had looked crushed, and the squawks emanating from the phone suggested she might be in trouble, which pumped up his protectiveness to eleven out of ten.

Why this had to happen today of all days he didn't know. It wasn't fair. Jess deserved a day off, and she'd finally looked like she was relaxing when her job had stolen her peace. Again. He knew she had trouble saying no, and he understood that, but he hated how her job had so many tentacles of expectation and obligation, threatening to crush the life from her. Going with her, doing what he could to protect her, felt like the least he could do. And yeah, escaping the tease and talk of weddings and babies—people living their best life when his had felt stalled— was a good reason, too.

The clouds above banked ominously, holding the faintest

sliver of green.

"We might get more snow," Cooper observed.

"Great."

Yep. She looked like she needed that like she needed a broken hip. Okay, not a topic to pursue. "Who else tried to call?"

"I don't know. You can check the phone messages. I felt so bad about ignoring the calls and now poor Starlight might not make it."

"Hey, you can't be everywhere all at once."

"I know that." Her voice held an edge.

Okay then. "Would you like me to listen to your other calls?"

"Excuse me?"

"I mean see which ones from the vet service might need attention, that's all."

She exhaled. "To be honest, I don't think I could concentrate on anything except Starlight right now. You can listen, I don't care." She shrugged. "And if there's anything that you think I really need to know about then tell me, but otherwise I'd rather not know. I'm trying to remember what I have to do."

So he listened, decided that the Jenner's chickens weren't a top priority, something confirmed on call five when Mrs. Jenner rang again and said they were doing better. The Rowlings' dog had a similar outcome, sick one minute, but when he phoned them back—after getting Jess's blessing—it was to learn that it was better now.

But the way Mr. Galbraith spoke to her, the tone of his increasingly terse and rude demands, concerned him. How dare someone speak to her this way? No wonder she was often so stressed and tense, if she had to take on board the emotions of others.

Then he heard the last call. "Hey Jess, this is Nick. I noticed you raced out before I could speak to you. Just wanted you to know I had a great time on Friday night and I really hope we can do it again soon."

He inhaled sharply.

"Who was that?" she asked, as she took a sharp turn into the Galbraith's gate.

"Your firefighter dude."

"Nick? What did he want?"

That was hardly the tone of someone madly in love. His heart flickered, dancing with hope. Maybe she wasn't. "Wanted to say he enjoyed Friday night and hoped to do it again."

She grimaced—okay, definitely not a look of love—but only said "Can you call Mr. Galbraith again and let him know we're almost there?"

He obeyed, and the farmer's shout of "About—" expletive "—time" made Cooper swallow a word. But Big Red was slowing down, stopping. Jess killed the engine, pulled on the handbrake, and grabbed her bag from the back.

"Hey," he called, holding up a coat that his mom had said she'd likely need.

She glanced back, then shook her head, hurrying to the barn.

He'd bring it anyway. Mom had also insisted he take a beanie and gloves for Jess, in case she hadn't brought her own. Knowing Jess, she probably had a whole wardrobe of clothes packed in that other bag she stored for emergencies. She was organized that way. Even if she'd seemed tense all the way here.

He closed her door with the requisite slam, then hurried inside the barn, from where he could hear a panicked voice.

"...don't understand why you didn't come here hours ago," Galbraith roared. "That's your job. Didn't you take a Hippocratic oath?"

"That's for medical doctors, Mr. Galbraith," she said calmly, as she stroked the horse. The young horse whinnied, butting her hand away as he nudged his stomach.

"Which you're supposed to be for animals," he snapped back. "I can't believe you didn't come here sooner."

Jess stood silently, checking the horse's gums then feeling

the colt's stomach, before listening to it with a stethoscope. The way she focused on the animal, ignoring the accusations being flung at her, impressed Cooper. He didn't think he'd have that same level of self-control.

Proved, when Galbraith started again, and Cooper snapped "She was with me."

Jess glanced at him, frowned, then returned her attention to the rear of the horse as the farmer continued his tirade. "I just bet she was. And I can imagine just what the two of you were—"

"At church, then with my family," Cooper said, pitching his voice low and controlled. He could take a leaf out of Jess's playbook. "And you should know how bad the phone reception can be around here."

Galbraith's cheeks reddened. "Are you saying you didn't get my calls?"

Obviously not, Sherlock, otherwise they wouldn't be here, would they? He bit his tongue, figuring the farmer probably didn't need that observation.

"Have you medicated Starlight?" Jess asked the farmer, ignoring his question.

"Of course I have. I had to, seeing there was no vet willing to come."

She pressed her lips together, and yet somehow Cooper heard the faintest sigh. "You know that medication masks clinical signs." She peered at him sharply. "Have you been walking him?"

"Yes!"

"Giving him water?"

"Yeah."

"Has he eaten anything?"

"No. So, is it colic?"

"I think so, but I need to check a few more things to know for certain."

"Maybe you would be certain if you'd been here when I first

called." Galbraith swore. "I wish your father was here. He'd know what to do."

Cooper saw the way her lips twisted, as if she was holding back her protest. He moved closer. "What can I do, Jess?"

She glanced at him, then at the farmer. "You've checked his feed?"

"First thing I did."

"Got any stools for me to see?"

Stools? Oh. Feces. Fun.

"I couldn't see any."

She glanced at Cooper. "Can you go find a sample of the horse's poo in the yard?"

Really? Gross. "Sure."

"Take your flashlight, it's getting dark out there."

"Am I looking for anything in particular?"

"If you find any, bring it here so I can see."

Awesome. "Sure thing, boss."

"Boss?" Galbraith said, looking between them.

"Thanks Cooper," she said, dismissing him.

He followed the farmer's direction outside, and used his phone's light to illuminate the ground. It was getting dark, and there was moisture hitting his face, like snow was about to fall. Man, he could think of a hundred things he'd rather be doing right now, but—

No. This is what he wanted to do. He wanted to help her.

He found a sample, scooped it up with the shovel Galbraith had provided, then took it inside.

A thrashing sound came from the stall, as the horse tried to kick at its stomach. "Here you go."

Jess kept her focus on the animal, ignoring the way its head thumped her, like it didn't want her touching it. "Steady, boy."

Again, he found himself admiring her, her patience, her calmness, the way her soothing touch brought peace to the situation. Unlike Galbraith, whose anxiety only seemed to transmit agitation to all creatures around.

"What does it look like?" she asked Cooper.

Wow. He definitely hadn't trained for this. He peered at the deposit on the shovel's blade. "Uh, I think it's dry? Except it's damp because it's trying to sleet out there."

She winced. Glanced at him. He moved the shovel closer so she could see. She peered at it, nodded. Then moved to her bag of tricks.

"We're going to do a nasogastric intubation, which means I'll need your help with a stomach tube."

"Sure."

He drew close, and put on gloves as she requested, then followed her instructions as she passed a tube through the horse's nose.

"What does this do?" he asked quietly.

"The tube goes down the esophagus and draws off the stomach contents. If there's a large amount of undigested food then we know whatever is causing the colic is preventing the stomach contents from passing through the digestive tract."

The next hours passed in more unpleasantness, but eventually the horse's heart rate lowered, and seemed to calm after medication was administered.

He was exhausted by the time Jess pronounced herself satisfied. How did she do this? She was incredible.

"It looks like there's no dehydration, but you'll need to watch him carefully until the colic signs subside, which should be in the next day or so. His appetite should return and he'll pass normal manure. You can do some controlled hand walks, but no grain until he's definitely showing improvement. And if there's any problems at all, then please call me."

Galbraith muttered something Cooper didn't quite catch, but Jess did, as she nodded.

"I don't know what to say," Galbraith muttered.

How about sorry to Jess, Cooper longed to say. But he didn't. Instead, he followed her instructions and cleaned up, stowed equipment in Big Red, then waited. Sure enough, the earlier predictions of snow saw spits of white drifting in the wind as a wall of gray approached, which seemed to be increasing by the minute. Jess and Mr. Galbraith talked, then the farmer finally stuck out his hand and she shook it.

"Jess, do you want me to drive?" he asked as she finally drew near.

She shook her head, but he could see she was weary, her shoulders slumped.

"Are you sure?"

She glanced at him from under heavy lids. "If it makes you feel better, then okay."

It would make him feel better. And likely her, too. She looked exhausted.

He opened the passenger door for her and she slid in. He closed it then jogged around to his door.

"I know you've always loved driving this thing," she said.

"Look, sportscars are fun, but Big Red has grunt."

"Sure does."

He steered back onto the road, the headlights' twin beams staring into the storm. Outside was dark, the snowfall getting thicker, forcing him to go slower as the tires slipped. They were miles from anywhere, no human habitation in sight, and this was not the place to get stuck. Then the vehicle shuddered, and he gripped the wheel harder as Jess gasped.

The snowstorm suddenly changed gear as the wind battered the vehicle. Here, on top of a mountain in east Washington, they were prime targets for whatever ornery weather vagaries might seek to attack, and this looked like they were heading straight into a blizzard which was sweeping in on top of the ridge.

"Lord, keep us safe," he prayed aloud, to Jess's loud "Amen."

Then the vehicle skidded and jerked and the engine died.

CHAPTER EIGHT

"What's happened?" Jess leaned over to look.

Cooper stabbed the starter. "It's not going."

No joke. "I knew I should've driven."

"Hey, you're welcome to come over here and make it go."

But the blizzard outside meant getting out of the vehicle to prove a point wasn't helpful. "Look, Big Red is a lady, you just have to treat her right. So put your foot on the accelerator gently, and—"

"I know how to drive, Jess."

"Yeah? Well, I don't know why we're stuck here then, if that's the case. Oh wait, you only know how to drive expensive imports these days, right? I forgot."

"That's uncalled for."

"Don't get me started," she warned, then slumped in her seat. Frustration steamed over her as she fought the inclination to kick him out from the driver's seat. He'd driven Big Red many times in the past; he'd know if something was wrong. Ergo, something was wrong. Very wrong. And they were stuck here in a snowstorm miles from anywhere, and all she wanted was to find her own bed. What a day.

She drew out her phone. "I'm gonna see if I can call—oh."

"No reception?"

"Not a bar."

"Cell coverage is always patchy around here. Do you have a two-way?"

"It's getting repaired." Just another thing in the long list of to-do's that she'd forgotten to check.

"I could trek back to the farm," he offered.

"You know as well as I do that the safest thing to do is stay with the truck. The way this storm is carrying on you could get lost or even freeze before you're halfway there."

"So it looks like we're here for the night."

Awesome. She was so tired, tears felt but one wrong word away.

"Hopefully it'll blow over soon then the phone signal will work again," he said more gently.

"Yeah." *Please God.* She scrubbed her face and groaned. "I should've got there earlier. If I'd checked my phone I would've gone straight there and it wouldn't have taken so long and I'd be home now, not stuck here with you."

She heard how ungracious those last words sounded, bouncing around the truck's cabin. It was so dark she couldn't see his face, but she didn't want to hurt him. He'd been so kind to her after all. "I didn't mean to sound like that."

"I know what you mean." His tone was relaxed, unoffended. "Jess, you were taking a necessary break."

If only. "I wish."

"When was the last vacation you took?"

"Vacation? What's that?"

He sighed. Turned to face her.

She could glimpse that from the weird light coming through the windshield. She looked away.

"Don't tell me you haven't had a vacation since that time we went to Disneyland."

She pressed her lips together. Very well. She wouldn't.

"Jess."

His voice was low, raspy, and did unnerving things to her heart. "Thank you for your help today."

"I meant it before. Any time."

"Except that's not true, is it?"

"What do you mean?"

"You'll get another job, you'll move far away, and I won't see you anymore."

Space stretched between them, her unasked questions falling into the silent moments between wind shrieks and thudding snow.

"Do you want to see me?" he asked softly.

Yes. No. He—this—scared her.

"I want to see you," he murmured.

She pivoted to face him, but it was so dark now she couldn't see him. But flicking on a phone torch wasn't going to answer what she sensed he really meant right now.

"Jess, it killed me to see you with Firefighter Dick the other day."

She almost-smiled. "His name is Nick, Cooper."

"I don't care. He's not right for you. He doesn't know you like I do. He can *never* know you like I do. He's not right for you, Jess."

"I know."

"And can't you see—wait. You know that?"

"Yes." Somehow it felt easier to speak the truth in the dark.

"But you went out with him. Or stayed in with him. I mean, I hope you didn't do that—"

"He left not long after you did. It was a thank-you dinner after he helped me clean the kitchen after the fire, that was all."

"Oh."

Seconds ticked away. Seconds when she could mount back on the high horse of offense, or stay in this softer place and be honest and finally say some of those things that really needed to be said.

Lord? Please help me.

She sucked in a breath, silently exhaled. Here went nothing, then. "I… I felt so bad," she admitted, "because you'd been so kind and helpful, then when you showed up I really wanted to kick Nick out and eat pizza with you like we used to."

She felt her hand grasped, and she curled her fingers around his.

At once a million images sprang to life. The way they used to spend school afternoons together, studying math, working on chemistry. She'd been a happy nerd with him, taking out science fairs, winning science and math contests. Then their studies had seen them in Seattle for a time, before he'd completed his studies then his masters on the other side of the country. Those years apart had been hard, but had forced them to get intentional about connecting. So by the time he'd returned, it had only been a matter of time as they'd danced around taking things further, until Jackson and Lexi's engagement party when they'd finally gotten serious, sealing things with a kiss.

Her fingers tightened. She remembered Cooper's kisses, in all their glorious rainbow technicolor. She'd always thought that he'd been perfect for her, so smart, kind and gentle. Until he wasn't.

She stilled, as the memory of last May swallowed the others. Their fight. At the reopening day for the Trinity Lakes' historical museum.

His words were burned in her brain. "You could do so much better than this. Think what your life could be if you weren't stuck in this small town."

"But I love it," she'd insisted. "I love what I do. Why would I want to leave?"

"Because I don't want you to stay. I want you with me. You could see more of the world like Ellie did."

"But I don't want to travel. I'm a small-town girl. I like it here."

He'd held her hand. "But what if I want you with me?"

"What are you saying?" Part of her had wondered if he was subtly proposing. But then his next words had killed that.

"I'm going back to California. You could come with me."

"And what?" His lack of explanation was frustrating. "Live with you?"

"No."

"Then what? Hang around in the background waiting for a drop of your precious spare time? You're a workaholic, Cooper."

"So are you."

"I know that," she'd snapped. "I also know that I could never leave my dad's clinic. He had a heart attack not so long ago, in case you don't remember."

Cooper had only stared at her, his lack of response drawing deeper frustration.

"Let me get this straight: you think the answer is for me to leave my family, my work, my town, all of which I love, and what—go and live with you?"

The fact he never said anything more was what killed her. He'd basically blamed her for having the exact same work tendencies as he had, then said her actions hurt him.

She'd flared into anger. "I can't believe you can say stuff like this! I can only wonder why. You've always been about Cooper first. You don't consider me or what I want to do at all."

"But I am. I can see all your work is stressing you out, and I care too much to see you burn out."

He'd tried to hold her hand, but she pulled away. "I might've once thought that you cared about me, but it's obvious this won't work out."

"Jess—"

"No. Don't look at me like that. I should've realized this years ago. We're too different."

"We're not."

"We are if you want your rich, city life and I'm staying here. I can't do this anymore, Cooper. We're done."

And she'd turned and walked away.

Now, she wondered if she should've given him another chance. If she should've answered his messages, answered the door. Listened to her parents who had wanted her to patch things up. But, as Ellie had said later, Cooper had needed to return to work—of course! And she'd been so embarrassed and self-conscious about being on show to half of Trinity Lakes that trying to patch things up hadn't been high on her list of priorities back then.

But it was now. "I'm sorry about last year."

He squeezed her hand. "Me too." He sighed. "I'm so sorry for hurting you. I had so many things to say, I'd practiced it, and wanted to sound smooth, but instead I messed things up so bad."

"What did you want to say?" she whispered.

"That I'm in awe of you. That I think you're incredible, and I always have. Even in college I never noticed anyone else. It was all you, with your heart and your looks and your brain."

She bit her lower lip to stop its wobble.

"I know I sounded selfish last year in saying you should come with me, and yeah, on reflection, it probably was. But I couldn't see any other option for you to escape the obligations of working here."

"But what if I don't want to escape?"

"Don't you?" he asked gently.

Okay, if the truth was really told, she *was* tired, so very tired of doing this, of feeling like she had to live up to the family legacy. Martin's Veterinary Services had been an institution in Trinity Lakes for three generations. She did feel a sense of family obligation to continue. But doing this alone these past two weeks had shown how hard it was. "Okay, sometimes I feel like I'd like to do something else."

"Like what? What would you do if you could do anything in the world?"

She thought about it for a long moment. Travel? Maybe. Get married, have a family? Yes. But only if she was sure she'd be there to see her husband, and he her. And no way could she have children with this current pace of life. And as saying that felt too impossible, there was only one answer. "I don't know."

"I'm not saying quit your work here, but I hate the way you're worn so thin by all these people who speak so poorly to you and treat you as their punching bag."

"I can take a hit."

"But you have to take so many of them. Every day. Without getting a chance to regather and be refreshed and get your physical and emotional strength back. Jess, I…"

He paused, and her heart teetered on a pinnacle of hope, as she wondered what he was going to say.

"I'd hate to see you reach a point where you burn out and can't continue."

Oh. Not *I love you*? She swallowed disappointment. Why should he suddenly say those words now when he'd never said them before? "I'd hate to see that too."

His grip tightened. "Then when your dad comes back, can you talk with him, see if he wants to take on a partner? It's got to be hard on him too."

It was. She knew that. And maybe all these vacations were her father's way of making up for lost time. A heart attack was one way of reprioritizing life. "I can talk to him."

But talking to him was one thing. What did reducing her hours mean if Cooper got work elsewhere? She didn't want to live in some big city, pandering to the rich with their designer dogs.

She shivered, and her teeth chattered.

"You're cold."

She drew her coat across her more tightly. "I can't believe how quickly the weather changed."

"It's what it does up on these high ridges. With any luck it'll blow away soon and we'll get our phone signal back."

"Can't wait."

Although it was nice to be here, spilling secrets, sharing truths, getting the sense that past wounds were finally having a chance to be healed and restored. Even if she was getting cold. And—her stomach growled—hungry.

"Oh man."

Her cheeks heated. Apparently embarrassment was one way to keep warm. "Sorry about that."

"No, with all you've gone through you are completely entitled to feeling hungry. I can't believe I forgot until now."

"Forgot what?"

"Mom sent some leftovers."

"Really?"

"She's a fan of yours. I know she wants us to get back together."

"You think? I wasn't sure, not with all the ever-so-subtle hints, like forcing you to come work with me. Then feeding me the most delicious pastries in the world."

"Yeah, us Reillys don't do subtle well."

Except some did. For all Cooper's talk before, she still wasn't sure where she stood with him. Her stomach protested again. "So where is this food?"

He winced. "In the cooler out the back."

"Are you kidding? So it will be frozen now."

"Probably."

"Wow. That's almost as bad as someone saying I thought I'd get you flowers but I didn't."

"Except I did," he pointed out.

"And they were beautiful," she murmured.

"So you liked them?"

"Of course I did."

"And Fireman Sam didn't give you any?"

"No."

She could feel the satisfaction emanating from him. Then she shivered again.

"Hey, Mom sent a jacket for you."

"Is that outside too?"

"Nope. That one is in here." He leaned behind and drew it out.

She tucked it over her legs. She sure hadn't planned to get trapped in a snowstorm when she'd chosen to wear these jeans this morning. "Thanks." Her teeth chattered again. "So, uh, what was in the cooler?"

He sighed. "Would you hate me if I said ribs?"

She closed her eyes. "No." But now she could imagine them, could almost taste them, and her mouth salivated at the memory of how tasty Jackson always made them. "I really hope there aren't any wolves out there who can smell those ribs."

"Pretty sure they wouldn't be game to mess with Big Red." He sighed. "You really want them, huh?"

"I'm really hungry," she admitted. She might've stuffed herself at lunch, but work like this tonight always fueled her appetite.

"Okay, I'll be your hero. Wait here."

"What? No—"

But it was too late as he'd opened the door and shut it, the extra force in closing perhaps due to the icy wind.

Oh my goodness. She hoped he knew enough to hold onto Big Red's sides and work his way back. She switched on the phone torch and held it as feeble light for him as she peered through the back glass. But between the dark and the snow she could see nothing. How was she ever going to explain things if he died in a snowstorm just because she was hungry?

The door beside her opened with a jerk and she squealed.

"Move over," he instructed, and she scooted closer to the middle as he leaned across and placed a cooler between her and the passenger door. He then clambered in afterwards, shutting the door, as he sat close to her. Snow dusted his hair and eyelashes, and she was sorely tempted to draw her hand down his cheeks. She didn't.

His fingers were stiff, and she helped him undo the plastic clasps and retrieve the wrapped food. "It's still warm."

His teeth glinted in the darkness. "God bless Mom."

"Amen."

She didn't care that the ribs were barely-warm; they tasted like manna, and even more delicious this time around. There were even two chocolate cupcakes for dessert.

"Feel better now?" he asked, as she followed it with a swig of water from her bottle.

"I never thought I'd do a picnic in the middle of a winter snowstorm with you."

"It's good to try new things, though, right?"

Some things. "Sure."

"I'm gonna go shift this back out—"

"No, you'll only get colder, and let more cold air in here." She picked up the cooler's handle. "I'll stick it on the floor—"

"Put in on the driver's side."

"Are you staying over here?"

"It's gonna get colder, Jess, so we should stay close together."

She swallowed. It was one thing to be trapped with him in a vehicle. It was quite another to be snuggling up with him. But she followed his instructions, carefully lifting the cooler across the gear stick and brake and placing it on the seat, as he retrieved a blanket from the storage compartment behind the seats.

He rubbed the side of her arm. "You're cold. Come here." He

handed her the beanie his mom had found, and she put that on too, then he helped her into her jacket.

"Is your mom a prophet or something? How did she know we'd need all this?"

"She's pretty smart."

He shifted, stretching out his legs while encouraging her to stretch hers toward the back of the driver's seat. He draped the blanket over her, checked she was warm and tucked in, then moved so her head could rest against his chest, his arms holding her securely. Outside the storm continued, with wind gusts rattling the vehicle, and icy breath stole through the vents.

But inside, she was thankful for the bench seat that allowed them to rest like this. Here, in his arms, his heart beating with strong reassurance.

And the thought that even though there might still remain so much uncertainty, right now, here in his arms she was safe.

———

HE'D SCARCELY DARED dream about this moment. That he'd finally get to hold Jess in his arms again. That bridges felt mostly mended. And sure, being stuck in a snowstorm wasn't part of the dream, but it was worth it to hold her. To remember how she fit perfectly with him, in his arms and in his life, and to breathe in her scent, the essence that made Jess everything he loved.

He should've said that earlier. Should've said it back last May. That the reason he cared for her so much was because she was the only woman for him and always had been. How could he care about anyone when he'd found the star and knew that only she would do?

He tugged her closer, smoothing her soft hair with his hand until the cold begged him to draw on gloves. It wasn't surprising nobody was out here. Chances were they'd be undiscovered until morning, so they'd do well to stay huddled close, and stay warm as best they could. And he'd dream that one day this could happen without a snowstorm. Like after a wedding like his sister's. If God so willed. Which reminded him…

Hey Lord, it feels like a miracle to be holding her again. Help me show her she can trust me. And please keep us safe, and guide our paths.

He woke to silence, but to the strangest eerie light on the horizon, like a green crackle across the sky. He smeared away the fogged-up window. Blinked. Then tapped his phone. Still no signal, but it was nearly two in the morning. Was that—?

"Hey, Jess." He nudged her.

"Cooper," she murmured, her eyes closed, before snuggling closer.

His heart clenched. What he'd give for the chance to do this every night. He'd barely slept, not just because of their uncomfortable position, but because it seemed every sense had flared to life when she was so near. And while he didn't want to spoil her sleep, he knew she'd want to see this.

"Jess? Wake up. There's something you should see."

"What?" She dragged a hand down her face, and rubbed her eyes like a little kid.

He smiled. "Hey." He wrapped his arm around her shoulder and helped her sit up. "Look out the front." He wiped away more of the condensation, glad the snow hadn't piled too high on the truck's hood.

"What am I looking at?"

"See out there?" He pointed to the line of green that wavered and rippled high in the sky.

"Is that—?"

"The Northern Lights? I think so."

"Oh wow!"

The green ribbon wisps billowed and danced in the wind. Every so often their breath would fog the windshield and they'd wipe it off, ready to watch more. He did his best to capture a photo, using his latest model phone, but photos could never do this justice.

"I didn't think you could see them so far south," she murmured.

"I've heard stories of people catching glimpses from California, even Texas. It's more about having the right conditions, about when the solar activity and conditions are right."

"It looks like lava coming from a volcano," she said. "I can't believe that when we went to sleep it was snowing, and now the skies are clear enough to see this."

"The wind must have blown all the clouds away."

"And God wanted to give us a special gift."

"Amen." It felt incredibly special, a privilege to watch this. He didn't know anyone else in Trinity Lakes who had ever seen the lights like this before. But then, the town was situated down lower, and even the ranch was perched lower too. Up here on top of a mountain with no light pollution, with only stars illuminating the snowy mountain ranges spread like a rumpled blanket before them, proved the perfect conditions.

"It's a gift on the other side of a storm," she said softly.

He wondered if she was talking about the blizzard, or if she meant something else. For holding her, being with her like this, sure felt like a God-given gift. Something that they could've missed, or given up on, but now it felt like a promise, as much as any rainbow that God would never flood the earth again.

She snuggled closer, and he drew her near, and they watched until the lights finally disappeared. "Thank you for waking me to see that."

"It was pretty special." He traced her cheek with his gloved hand. "A special moment with a special lady."

Her cheeks pushed up as she smiled before she ducked her head and laid it on his chest again.

He liked her feeling comfortable with him. He loved how she wriggled until she snuggled in. He'd like nothing more than for her to do this the rest of his days.

"What's the time?" she asked sleepily.

"Nearly three. We should get some rest."

"Does the phone have any signal?"

He glanced at it. "Not yet."

"Hopefully it will in the morning."

He pressed a kiss to her forehead. "Get some sleep."

"You too."

But the way she snuggled in, her curves against his frame, meant he knew he'd struggle to sleep any more.

He composed a text to Jackson, and pressed send, but was unsurprised when it failed to send. But if the signals returned, maybe it would pick up, and transmit across the night skies just like the aurora borealis had done.

He wrapped her closer, and closed his eyes.

And when next he awoke it was to hear a muffled yell and see Jackson's face pressed against the window.

CHAPTER NINE

Voices woke her. Someone shifting. The beautiful dream—tropical sunsets, she and Cooper dancing—dissipated as she blinked and worked to get her bearings. Where—? What—? Oh!

"Morning, Jess," Jackson Reilly grinned at her.

Jackson? She straightened, pressing against something firm which drew an "Easy there, Doc," from Cooper.

Her cheeks heated as she realized she'd been pressing against his leg. "Sorry."

"It's okay." He smiled. "How are you doing?"

"I feel like I can't tell if this is real or not." She righted her beanie—her hair would be such a mess—and looked at Jackson. "What are you doing here?"

"Being the knight in shining armor."

"I sent him a text," Cooper explained. "It finally got through."

"So I'll take you back to the ranch."

"You can get through?"

"The storm looks like it was worst up here. I don't know if they'll have seen much beyond a snowfall down in Trinity Lakes."

The clinic! "What's the time? I need to get to work."

"It's nearly seven," Jackson said.

"You can take a day off," Cooper said.

But if she took a day off she'd get behind again. And she already felt so behind that she didn't want to add any more pressure to her life. "I don't think I can."

"Hey," Cooper shifted to face her, his eyes serious. "Remember what we talked about? If you keep working so hard you'll burn out, and I don't want to see that."

"But I can't let people down."

"Which you will if you burn out," Cooper said softly.

"That's right," Jackson said. "Because who will look after the animals then?"

Oh. She bit her lip. She thought Cooper meant she'd disappoint him if she burned out. He probably only meant what his brother said.

"Come on. Let's get you two in my truck and get you back."

She grabbed her essentials and exited Big Red into wind so cold it stole her breath. Fortunately Jackson's huge vehicle was parked nearby, and she hopped inside while the two men spent a few minutes working to jump start Big Red. Jess wasn't such a feminist that she needed to be out there too. Big Red wouldn't go, so it wasn't too long until they had joined her in the warm vehicle.

"Sorry Jess, but it looks like you'll need a tow truck."

"And a snow plow."

"But how will I get to the farms tomorrow?"

"Leave that, we'll sort that out when we get back."

But she couldn't. It was like the hours of enforced rest meant her brain was now way too ready to kick into high gear and think about all the things she had to do. Like the prohibitive costs of a new vehicle—or at least a hefty towing charge and repair bill. Catching up on missed appointments. Seeing all the

—

"Just breathe, Jess," Cooper said.

"I am breathing."

"Stop worrying. We'll sort this."

We would? Did that mean he planned to stick around? But before she could chase that rabbit trail Cooper wrapped her hand in his, stealing comprehension.

Didn't he mind that Jackson had noticed, and was now smirking?

"So, uh, how did you know where we were?"

"Cooper's message," Jackson said.

Oh, right. He'd said that. She yawned.

Cooper nudged her. "We'll get you home, you can have a shower and see how you feel about working today."

"You'll take me to Trinity Lakes?"

"Jackson will drive us back to the ranch—he's got things to do—and I'll drive you there."

"Thank you."

"If you like I can see about getting Big Red towed," Jackson offered. "We might be able to get it to the ranch, then it's not gonna cost as much."

"That's really kind. Thank you."

"No worries."

Cooper shifted, and her head fell on his shoulder. "Hey, close your eyes and you can rest for a bit, okay?"

She didn't need a second invitation. She'd tried to sleep as best she could, but she'd been all too conscious of Cooper's warmth, his body so close to hers. Then that magical moment of watching the Northern Lights together, followed by the dream when she'd imagined they were honeymooning on a tropical island, and…

"Hey, we're here," Cooper murmured, drawing her awake, which was emphasized as Jackson shut the door with a huge slam.

"Do you want to have breakfast here or go straight back to town?"

She wanted—needed—to get back to the vet clinic.

"Silly question. I can see your answer on your face. Okay, come in and get warm by the fire while I grab Mom's keys. I think she's planning on staying here today, and I'd rather use her car than mine on snow."

She entered the Reilly ranch and was instantly swallowed in a hug by Beth Reilly while Cooper disappeared down the hall. Probably to change.

"I'm so glad you're okay," Beth said. "We figured you and Coop would be safe—you're such a sensible girl after all—but a mother still worries. Now, are you hungry? Need a shower? Want a coffee?"

"I am, and I really do, but I'll wait until I get back into town. I don't want to be late."

"The coffee is ready now, so here you go." She poured a mug and added milk, and passed it to her.

Jess sipped it. "Oh, this is heaven."

Beth smiled.

"And thanks so much for packing those ribs for us yesterday. That was very welcome as our dinner."

"You poor things. Are you sure I can't tempt you with some oatmeal or toast?" She cocked her ear. "I think Cooper's having a shower so there is time."

He was? Didn't he know she had to get to town? Oh. But maybe he was doing that because he thought he was going to work today too. The fact he'd do that for her made her blink hard. She took another sip, then glanced at her phone as it buzzed with a message. Mr. McAffrey, needing an urgent appointment for one of his rescues. A squirrel, it seemed this time. She sighed.

"You're not going to work today, are you?" Beth asked.

Jess held up her phone. "I'm already getting messages from people. I can't afford to take a day off."

"You can't afford to get sick, young lady. You need to learn to prioritize your health, too."

Jess nodded, sipping her coffee and making small talk with Beth as they waited for Cooper. Within five minutes he was there, dressed in jeans and a t-shirt. Well, hello. His damp, dark curly hair and unshaved face that said he'd run out of time perked her senses to awareness as much as any first caffeinated drink of the morning.

He smiled, and her heart thudded hard again.

"Did you tell Mom about the Northern lights?"

"What?" His mother's jaw sagged. "You didn't see them with that storm, did you?"

"We did, after the storm passed. It was spectacular."

"I didn't think you could see them around here," Jess confessed.

"Here's a picture," Cooper said, showing his mom his phone.

"Oh my word! It is remarkable." Beth glanced at Jess. "Peter Franklin will be so envious. He loves the stars and night skies."

"Well, now we know it can be seen there, maybe we could add it to the ranch stay options." Cooper shrugged.

"Ooh, that's a good idea."

He glanced at Jess. "You ready to go?"

She nodded. This interlude was nice, but she was now itching to return.

"Hey Mom, can I swap cars with you today?"

"You mean I'll need to use your fancy sports car to go visit the chickens?"

He mock-sighed. "If you must."

"You take care of this one," Beth said to Cooper. "She's precious cargo."

His eyes turned to Jess. "I know."

Her heart skipped several beats. Maybe she hadn't misunderstood things. Maybe what she'd wondered might be a dream had actually been true. His eyes certainly seemed to be saying that he wanted her to give him a second chance.

She swallowed, put the coffee mug down. "Thanks, Mrs. Reilly."

"Beth, please." Cooper's mom hugged her again. "Get some sleep, and don't work too hard, okay?"

"Yes, ma'am."

She followed Cooper out to the hall where they donned their thick coats and scarves again, then outside to his mom's new vehicle. She'd bought it brand new after Ellie's fake French boyfriend had stolen Beth's car and crashed it last year.

The drive down into Trinity Lakes was quiet, the countryside stunning with the fresh snowfall. What a contrast the past twenty-four hours had proved. Not just in the landscape, either.

She peeked across as Cooper drove. Things with him felt… better. Much better than she could've imagined. Almost like God had answered her prayer with one of His "above all she could ask or imagine" promises.

He glanced at her. "Are you doing okay?"

She nodded. "I'm tired, but I bet you are too."

"You can rest your eyes if you like. I don't want you to get sick."

Neither did she. He was right. There was no wiggle room for sickness, she had to protect her own health.

She tried to rest her eyes, but kept peeking up to see where they were so that it was just easier to keep them open. They passed the Trinity Lakes Bible college where Lexi's parents lived and worked, passed the waterpark, closed until summer, then approached the Trinity Lakes sign. New landscaping on the town limits showcased the leafless poplars and 'Welcome to Trinity Lakes' sign to full advantage.

"Thank you for all you did, yesterday and last night, and

well, now." She swallowed. "I don't know what I would've done if I'd been out there alone."

"I don't know if I'd have coped knowing you were alone, either."

She glanced at him, but his attention was on the road as he turned off Main Street into Wainscott.

"Cooper."

He flicked her a look.

Her mouth dried. It seemed weird to say they needed to talk, when they'd spent so much time doing exactly that last night. And when she'd just forgone the opportunity to do so right now. But she needed clarity about just what he was thinking about them and the future. "Cooper, I..." Suddenly couldn't find the words.

He turned into the driveway and parked. "Jess, we'll talk, but right now you're here, and you've got half an hour until the first patient comes."

"Oh." Suddenly she didn't care about the clients. She just really wanted to know what he was thinking.

He pulled into her driveway and stopped the car. She exited, and a Northern Face-wearing Nick exited from next door.

"Jess? Oh, you're back. Thank goodness. You had me all kinds of worried. I was about to send out the search party." He glanced at Cooper. "Were you out with him?"

Cooper had stiffened. She placed a hand on his arm, noticed him relax.

"Thanks for your concern, but I'm fine and dandy. My truck died, and I've just come back from the Reilly's ranch." All true. "You've met Beth and Jackson Reilly at church, right?"

"Oh, right. Yeah."

"You'll have to excuse me. We've got work soon."

"He's still working with you?" Nick asked.

She looped an arm through Cooper's. "Yes, he is. And he's great at it. Now, please excuse me."

She opened the front door, and was met with a yowl of felines. "Oh, ladies! I'm so sorry. I forgot you didn't have dinner either."

"I'll deal with them while you have a shower."

"I smell that bad, huh?"

He smiled. "You could never smell bad to me."

Bless him. He even seemed serious.

Anne and Bess wove between her legs, and she leaned down to stroke them. "Hello, my little queens. I'm sorry I wasn't here last night. I hope you'll forgive me."

Bess meowed plaintively, and she picked her up. "Oh, poor baby. Did you think I'd forgotten you?"

"Looks like it."

"Now, don't be mean. She's the reason I've stayed sane as long as I have." She snuggled her face in the cat's ginger hair. "Bless you, Bess."

———

COOPER STILLED. "WHAT DID YOU SAY?"

"Bess?" She glanced up. "She's one of my cats. You've met her. I'm sure you have."

Yes, he had. On Dream Match. Now he looked more closely, he recognized the cat's face as the one BlessBess had posted in her jokey picture on the site. But didn't all cats look the same?

She put the cat down and toed off her shoes. Slipped off her socks. "Oh, that's better."

Maybe he'd got it wrong. Until he glanced down and recognized those toenails too.

She *was* BlessBess.

Oh man. How could he admit that he was BizC? He'd thought it cute, and appropriate. Business Cooper who was always busy. BizC.

What would she say when he admitted the truth? And why

was she looking at him soft-eyed like that while leaving poor BizC dangling on a string?

He didn't know what to do. Except say, "You probably should have that shower now."

Her nose wrinkled. "You're not exactly convincing me that I don't smell terrible."

"Of course you don't." Although he could feel himself sweating. He'd probably need another shower soon, too. How could he not have realized? How could he figure out how to take this forward without embarrassing her? Because he just knew she'd feel embarrassed. *Lord, what do I do?*

He continued to pray while she disappeared to get cleaned and changed, and he made her an omelet for breakfast. Something that would fill her up and keep her going for a while. And as he cooked, he contemplated how to admit the truth. But maybe it'd be okay. Sometimes in life you had to break a few eggs along the way.

She soon reappeared, and his mouth dried. Combed wet hair was a good look on her, and she didn't need makeup.

Her head tilted. "Are you doing what I think you are?"

Pretending he didn't know that she was BlessBess? He cleared his throat. "It depends on what you think I'm doing."

"Saving the day by making me my favorite omelet?"

Her smile hit him straight in the solar plexus. He needed to mention about Dream Match. He needed to admit—

"And you made coffee too?" she asked.

"Of course."

"Thank you." She held up the carafe. "Want one?"

"Sure."

Any chance for coffee or conversation was stolen as the doorbell buzzed and she sighed. "I thought I had more time than that."

"Stay here, eat, and I'll keep them in the waiting room."

"Thanks, Coop. You're a lifesaver."

Coop. He walked to the front door to admit the anxious arrival. She hadn't called him Coop since May. It made him feel like they could resume their relationship—if it wasn't for this pesky thing called Dream Match, and just what that signified. That he'd been seeking a new relationship. He winced. She might not take too kindly to that. But then, an inner voice argued, so had she, so she couldn't call him out when she'd done the same.

He kept puzzling the question as he welcomed Mr. Reynolds and commenced a long day of cats and dogs and birds and fluffy small pets and reptiles, punctuated by frequent yawns. The yawning got so bad after lunch he was desperate for a nap, but instead only had time to follow Jess's lead and snatch a banana muffin from the thank-you basket Mrs. Carrigan had made for Jess to thank her for her help with her "darling Teddy".

Confusion about what to say kept him quiet during the day. Instead, he juggled appointments, made decisions for Jess based on the urgency—and noise levels—of waiting cases, and in his quieter moments, explored ways of helping streamline her automated appointment scheduling and website so it wouldn't be so burdensome.

He also did what he could to help her with her vehicle, after Jackson called to say he'd towed it to the ranch, and Brandon from Trinity Lakes Auto was coming to look at it after-hours tonight.

"So he wants to know whether you want Big Red repaired, or whether you want to get a new car instead," he told her as they stole a quick mid-afternoon break to eat another muffin.

"Repaired, of course." She wiped at the crumbs on either side of her face. "You know why it's important to me."

Because it had been her grandfather's, and he'd used it for exactly the same reasons, visiting the farms and out-of-town properties when he'd been Trinity Lakes' vet a few decades ago. And while Coop might wish he understood family connection and heritage like that, he also knew maintaining the old sometimes came at a cost. Hence why he and Ellie and Jackson had never wondered too much about their dad. There was little point when they either barely or couldn't remember him.

"I know you're sentimental about Big Red, but one day she will need to retire."

"But she's been so good to me over the years."

"But if she's going to cost a bomb to fix, then maybe you need to consider if something newer with all the mod-cons would better suit your needs."

"I don't care about power windows."

"But in-built phone service could be useful, right?"

"Only if there's phone coverage." She folded her arms.

"You know you can get ones with satellite coverage too."

She glanced away.

"Look, how about I tell Jackson to keep the appointment and you get an estimate."

"Maybe I should just meet the mechanic. What time is the appointment?"

"When Brandon knocks off. So just after five."

She bit her lip. The vet clinic didn't close until six, and the past week of work had showed him that she rarely left before seven.

"You can trust Jackson. And Brandon too."

"I know. It's just…" She sighed.

"Hard to let go of control?"

She gasped. "Cooper!"

Not Coop anymore. "I get it. I really do." Nobody understood workaholism more than he. "But I also get that tendency to perfectionism that makes you such a good vet also has a downside, where you want to know everything and feel like you can control the outcomes. But the very nature of your work is that you can't control every outcome. Disease happens, accidents too. So sometimes you need to let others help you manage those things that aren't as important."

"Big Red *is* important."

"I understand that. But—"

"I don't think you really do. You took off from the ranch as soon as you could, and your family never really cared about family stuff the way we did."

"Yes, we did. My mom did the best she could to care for us five kids when Donald took off—"

"I know she did. I'm not casting aspersions on her."

"Kinda sounded like you did."

"I'm sorry."

"Anyway, you know it's a family ranch, passed down from one generation to the next—"

"Apart from your dad, who left and disappeared."

His fingers clenched. "You know we don't talk about him."

"Look, I don't mean to sound mean, but I'm just pointing out that yeah, while our families have some surface level similarities, it's also pretty different too. Martin's Veterinary Services is a family business, and we all wanted to do this and serve the community in this way, and—"

"And my family has run the Reilly ranch for generations. I don't see how that's different."

"But apart from Jackson and Ellie you all left. And your mom, God bless her, only stayed because she had to put a roof over your heads. She didn't really have a choice."

"You don't know that." His mom loved the ranch. "Anyway, she chose to marry him and live there."

"It's not the same as choosing to study veterinary science and choosing to practice in the small town, like my family has done."

His chest grew tight, and he chose his words with care. "I know you don't mean to make it come across like this, but you're almost sounding like you think you're better than us."

"I don't think that at all." Her eyes were wide. "I'm sorry if that's what I implied." Her voice softened. "But I do think that we care about our family heritage a little more than you do."

"I've never liked ranching."

"See?"

Why were they arguing about this? He'd felt a powerful sense of reconnection, and this didn't feel like the way to capitalize on that. But then, tiredness had a way of making a person lose their filter and feel a little punchy. "Come on, Jess. I don't even know why we're fighting about this. If you care about your Grandad's car so much then keep it. No skin off my nose. But you might want to rethink how much you love this job, because the longer I work here the more I realize it doesn't love you."

"What do you mean?"

"You need an assistant. Like another vet, not just an admin person."

"When Dad returns—"

"Your dad got sick because the stress of this work almost killed him. And he's not coming back to work on a permanent part-time basis. You can't keep doing this on your own, and your dad is going to be involved less and less over the coming years. So the time to plan for that is now, not when he is no longer around."

Her jaw sagged. "I can't believe you said that."

"The truth? Come on. You know you prefer honesty, so I'm giving it to you honestly."

The front desk bell dinged, offering a welcome escape. "I'll talk to you later."

Her lips pressed together, and he was glad they couldn't talk further now, as he was pretty sure he wouldn't want to hear any of the words she was obviously bottling up inside.

The rest of the afternoon passed in appointments, more yawning—their tiredness had contributed to their filter-free frankness—and sly questions from a couple of nosy clients about how late both of them had stayed up last night.

He was glad when six o'clock came and he could finally switch on his phone.

To find an email from a former client in London about an opportunity there.

London? His chest grew tight. Was this part of God guiding his steps? If so, did that mean God was guiding Cooper away from Jess? He'd prayed, but hadn't expected this…

His phone dinged with a new message, and he tapped it open. Then discovered a dozen missed calls from his brother and mom.

But when he tried to call there was no reply.

"Cooper?" Jess's brow wrinkled. "Is everything okay?"

"Um, I don't know. I need to get home."

"Sure." Her smile held uncertainty. "Thanks again for all your help."

"Any time."

Her smile lifted at that, but he realized how false a promise that could be. Because if he was in London, how could he help her? "I need to go. I'll message you about the car when I hear what Brandon says. If necessary, I can be your chauffeur tomorrow."

"Thank you. Sleep well tonight." She yawned. "I know I sure will."

He nodded, said goodbye to Jess, then drove home. His body might be screaming to sleep, but his mind and heart only knew turmoil that meant sleep was sure to be far away.

When he arrived there was no sign of Brandon. But alongside Big Red was a vehicle he didn't recognize. Huh. Who was here?

He opened the door. "Mom?"

"In here, Coop," Jackson called.

He walked down the hall to find his mom and brother in the kitchen with a strange man.

His mom looked up, she seemed pale. "Mom? What's wrong?"

She glanced at the man then back at him, her mouth opening and closing but saying nothing.

Jackson sighed heavily, a sound that seemed to draw up from his dirt-smudged socks. "Coop, this man reckons he's Donald."

"Donald?" Donald who?

His mom finally spoke. "He says he's your father."

CHAPTER TEN

"Here you go, ladies."

She refilled the bowls with premium kitty kibble and stroked Bess as she rubbed her head against Jess.

Here, in this space of quiet after a whirlwind of the past thirty-six hours, allowed time for her to finally calm, to reflect, to recall the highs and lows of the past day and previous evening.

Highs: that time watching the northern lights, feeling a curious sense of oneness with Cooper.

Lows: today, when exhaustion had caused her to speak to him too bluntly. She winced. How could she, Coop's friend, have been so insensitive to point out the differences between his family and hers? Especially when he'd gone out of his way to help her so much in these past days? But his words today had cut deep and made her think all afternoon, and now into the evening.

Did she work as a vet because she loved it or because of family obligation? She was prepared to admit that a big part of the reason she used Big Red was because it gave a sense of reassurance to locals that she possessed the same trustworthy skills of her father and grandfather. They'd been used to seeing the red truck come down their drives ready to save the day, and since she was a child she'd known she wanted to do that too. But would it really hurt if she had a different vehicle, and was known for herself and her own skills, rather than merely wanting to continue in her dad's legacy and not let down the family reputation?

And while she did love the smaller animal workload, if she was to be truly honest then she could admit it was a bit of a drain sometimes. The sheer volume plus all the emotional drama did steal into her sleep, keeping her awake for hours at night wondering, worrying, about what she could have done better. What would it be like if she had someone—not her father—who could take on some of the smaller animal work that would leave her free to do more cattle and equine work?

Farmers like Mr. Galbraith might be bluff and at-times gruff, but while they might get angry, they rarely cried over the loss of a cow or horse. And she enjoyed the problem-solving aspect of what their issues might be, as she had with Brutus a couple of years ago. That was far more interesting to her than coping with the emotional challenges of dealing with the owners of an overfed dog or a cat that had been tortured.

And Coop was right. She didn't want to admit it but Dad really wasn't in a place to do much more than an occasional day here and there. He needed to really commit to retirement for the sake of his health. Which left her—where?

She pressed against a headache she could feel forming behind her temple. How could she go forward in the family veterinary business, without burning out? Was it even possible?

She knew the statistics. She knew veterinarians were more at risk of suicide than nearly every other profession. She knew Coop was right to be concerned about her. And she knew that she was struggling mentally, and couldn't keep up this pace indefinitely. Something had to give, and like he'd said, she didn't want it to be her health.

She closed her eyes, her memories flicking to last year. He'd said what he'd said from concern for her. And now, with the benefit of hindsight, she could see he was right. She did need more balance in her life. Trying to live up to the family legacy hadn't done her many favors.

Fresh regrets gnawed. Last night had ended up feeling... special. But while their discussion in Big Red had led to her feeling like some of the past had healed, she wondered whether today's conversation about families had ripped open a new hole in their friendship. She'd known she'd been too tired to truly convey what she'd meant. Nobody should ever try to use exhaustion-laden words.

Except maybe ones like this. *I'm sorry if I sounded mean today,* she tapped out on her phone. *Put it down to a lack of sleep. But I do appreciate you.*

Her heart hovered with hope, willing him to answer, but there was no response. Hmm. She hoped he was okay. If nothing else, she'd kind of expected him to contact her about Big Red.

At least that was an issue she could do something about. She placed a call to Brandon.

"Hi Brandon. This is Jessica Martin. I was wondering if you've heard from Jackson or Cooper about Big Red."

"Ah, I took a quick look, and yeah. I'm afraid it looks like you'll need a new engine."

She closed her eyes. "I have a feeling that's not going to be cheap."

He gave an estimate that made her gasp.

"Look, if I can be blunt—"

Oh, she knew he could be.

"—I think you're better off buying a new truck. I understand it's got sentimental value, but maybe you're better off saving yourself a lot of trouble by getting something that's not so worn out." His voice softened. "I know it's not what you want to hear, but I wouldn't feel right advising you to keep spending money on something that will continue to break down."

She sucked in a breath. Slowly released.

"If you like, I can keep an eye out for something similar that might serve your needs."

"I…" *Won't lose self-control.* "I'd appreciate that. Thank you."

"It's all good."

"How much do I owe you?"

"You don't. Coop fixed it up already."

He had? She owed him even more. But considering he was rolling in money, she wouldn't feel too bad. She'd offer to pay, even though she knew he'd refuse. He was a good man. A good man she'd hurt today.

She spent a moment praying for him, then cleaned up, dealt with the cats, had another shower, all waiting to see if Cooper would reply to her earlier message. When he didn't reply after two hours, she went to bed. Then wondered if her dream match had sent anything.

Her nose wrinkled. It seemed wrong to still be on this dating app when she was hoping that things could pick up with Cooper again. But he hadn't said anything about moving here, and she knew he wasn't going to be here forever. So for a girl who liked to plan and know her options, maybe it was a good idea to not give it up just yet.

She sent another message. *How was your weekend?*

Nothing came back.

Honestly. What was with men these days?

So she plugged in her phone to charge, switched off the light, prayed, and tried to sleep.

. . .

Tuesday passed in Jess rescheduling her usual farm visits as she explained about Big Red's malfunction.

"She was going for a few decades so it's no surprise," Mr. Galbraith said. "I guess that's another reason why I'm glad Starlight is doing better, so you don't need to visit."

He wasn't the only one. A number of her other farmer clients scheduled for today said similar things.

"I long thought a tiny slip of a thing like you needed a better vehicle," Mr. Walker said.

He had?

Maybe Cooper and Brandon were right about Big Red, and instead of paying for Big Red's repairs she should be using the money for something that was built this century.

She wished she could talk to Cooper about it. But he seemed to have gone silent. Was he okay? She figured he'd send a reply when he was ready. And maybe he was having some work issues. Her heart panged. Maybe he'd been offered a job already. He probably didn't need her bothering him about Big Red. Besides, Brandon had sent the quote for repairs, and in looking that over, she was fairly sure he was right and it would be wasted money. It'd be good to tell Cooper that he was right.

But when Cooper didn't show up for work on Wednesday she started to worry. He'd finally sent a message—*family stuff going on, can't make it, sorry*—and she'd been gracious in her reply.

No worries. I hope everything is okay. If there's anything I can do please let me know.

Cooper's absence made her realize afresh just how much he did at the clinic, and again how right he had been. Having someone on the front desk dealing with patients made things so much smoother than when she was trying to do it all herself. The constant running in and out and sorting out payment methods while dealing with noise and impatient people proved again just what an important job her mom had done for Jess's dad these many years. So she needed not only a partner in the veterinary business, but an admin person as well. Mom might do it for a bit, but if Dad fully retired Jess would bet her bottom dollar that Mom would wish to retire too. Which was only fair.

Tuesday's enforced stay-at-home due to a lack of wheels at least meant she'd had time to catch up on some much overdue paperwork, and she'd realized again that finances were pretty tight. It was obviously a question she needed to discuss with her father anyway, but maybe if they took on a partner, found someone who might be willing to inject a sizeable financial contribution, then it could work. She now itched to talk to her parents, but as ever, their travel schedule and the time zone differences made that a challenge.

She checked her phone again. Still no word from Cooper. Dream Match: nothing new there, either.

She sent Cooper another text. *Hey, hope everything is okay. Available to talk if you want. Praying for you and your family.*

———

"WHO IS THIS GUY?" Mitchell exploded from the computer screen where the family video chat was happening. "I just don't understand why he'd feel the need to show up after all this time."

'Donald' had explained that. Said he'd been hit by a truck in New Mexico, had amnesia, then his memory had come back to him a few years ago. Cooper listened as Jackson repeated what had been said on Monday night.

"Did he have proof of any of that?" Dermott asked.

He'd had documents, a medical certificate from a hospital, an old drivers' license that Cooper could barely stand to touch. This gaunt gray-haired old man bore no witness in his memories. His mom had thrown out all their wedding pictures, so he'd been erased from their house. But she'd been shaken enough to entertain the possibility that he might be who he said he was.

"So why didn't he come when he first got his memory back?" Mitchell scowled.

"He said he was ashamed," Cooper said.

"So he should be." Dermott shook his head. "What kind of man treats his family like that?"

Cooper's phone pinged with a new message. Jess.

"Who's that from?" Jackson peered across the dining table to look.

"Is it Jess?" Ellie smirked.

"She's praying for us," he admitted.

"You haven't told her any of this, have you?" Mitchell asked.

"Nope. Nobody knows. Except us here, and… uh, him."

"I'm not even convinced he's genuine," Dermott said. "What kind of person shows up after twenty years?"

A desperate one.

"What does Mom say?" Mitchell asked. "She'd know best, as she was married to him. We were only kids when he walked out."

Mitchell had been eight. Dermott only twelve. Jackson five. Cooper didn't remember him—he'd been three—while Ellie had been a baby. Awesome father that one, leaving poor Mom to raise five kids on her own. They'd assumed Donald Reilly was dead—he'd been declared legally dead by the courts years ago—but now he was back.

Or was he?

"Mom doesn't know what to think," Jackson admitted, shooting Cooper a glance.

"She went back to bed and has barely emerged since."

"Oh no." Ellie looked like she might cry. "Okay, I'll be there as soon as I can."

"Don't you have some big important exam coming up?" Cooper asked. "You need to stay in Seattle, get that done first."

"He's right," Jackson said. "Lexi has the next few days off and she's been keeping a close eye on her."

"*Is* Mom okay?" Mitchell asked. "I mean, if I need to take some days off I'm sure my team would understand."

"She'll be okay. Just trying to come to terms with things."

"What is there to come to terms with? The guy is obviously an imposter."

"Says the man who didn't meet him," muttered Jackson.

"What was that?" Mitchell demanded.

"I never want to see him again," Dermott said flatly. "I don't care if he is related to us, I'm never going to forgive him."

"Well, you not seeing him shouldn't be a problem seeing you're all the way over there on the opposite side of the country," Jackson snarked.

"Aren't you supposed to forgive if you call yourself a Christian?"

Dermott scowled at Ellie's comment, which drew a laugh from Mitchell. "Yeah, isn't that what the Bible says?"

"The what?" Jackson asked. "Since when has the womanizing Mitchell Reilly been reading the Bible?"

Now it was Mitchell's turn to scowl. Oh, the fun family dynamics. "I object to being called a womanizer."

"I'm sure you do." Jackson crossed his arms.

"I haven't womanized for at least a year."

"Good for you," Ellie said sarcastically.

Cooper chuckled as Jackson grinned. "Is this because of a certain neighbor?"

"I don't know what you mean." Wait—were Mitchell's cheeks turning pink?

"So, Mitch, what's this about you and the Bible?" Cooper prompted.

"I, uh, might've studied it a bit lately."

Huh. "Well, that's good to hear."

Mitchell shrugged. "But that's not what we're having this

family meeting for." He leaned forward, his bearded expression intimidating. "What are you doing about this joker? What makes Mom think for a second that he might be the real deal?"

"You mean apart from the fact he called himself Donald Evan Reilly, and had a wedding ring with the date of their wedding engraved inside, and recalled all kinds of things about life with Mom that she seemed to believe?"

Mitchell dropped a soft curse. Looked like that Bible studying had some work to do.

Cooper sighed. "Such bad timing, too."

"I'll say," Ellie groaned. "I just wanted to get married and not have to think about him and now this happens."

"You don't need to invite him to your wedding. We don't know if he's even really him."

"I know that, but if I don't, then what does that make me look like?"

"Cautious?" Dermott suggested.

"He's right." Mitchell folded his arms. "Don't go panicking because some guy says he's our father. You need to find out for sure."

"Like with DNA?"

"How do you find out about that?"

"Would Lexi know?" Ellie asked.

"She's not here at the moment, otherwise I'd ask her."

"Who else would know?"

Cooper's phone pinged with the reminder of the message that had just come through. His heart clenched. "I know someone who might be able to help us."

"Who?" Mitchell asked.

"I'll talk to Jess Martin."

———

"Are you serious?" Jess sank down in the chair. No wonder Cooper had called it a family emergency when he called earlier. This was three-siren worthy.

"Nobody apart from the immediate family knows, and it needs to stay that way."

"I'm not going to tell anyone," she assured.

"It's all so awful," he confessed.

Her heart broke for him. For the Reilly family. And after all she'd said about his family not being like hers... "I'm so sorry. I mean, would it be a good thing if he was your dad?"

"No."

"Why don't you contact Sheriff Thompson? He'd have a way of finding out if the man is an imposter."

"We wondered if you might know anything about how to match DNA."

Her eyes widened. "I'm hardly a research laboratory."

"But you'd know people, right? You'd be able to find out if someone could help."

She exhaled. "I think your best bet is still the sheriff. I don't think he'd go blabbing everything around."

"The others don't want anyone else to know. It's got the potential to get really messy. Jackson is freaking out. He's not convinced that this so-called Donald is our father either, but he wants to make sure. Especially since Jackson was the one who pushed to have him declared legally dead."

She winced. She remembered that time. But it had been the only way the Reilly family could move forward. Everyone in Trinity Lakes had agreed.

"It's going to be hell on wheels if he really is alive, especially after all that Jackson has done for the ranch, and all the hours he's worked there."

She winced. So true. "But even so, that wouldn't change the court ruling, would it?"

"We don't know. Mitchell said he'd talk to a lawyer, so we're waiting to find out."

"I really feel like you need to wait until you can follow the right legal channels. Because how are you going to get a sample from him? It needs to be handled cleanly, not be contaminated."

"I don't know. What's the best way?"

"I'm an animal doctor, Coop. Not a member of the CIA."

"What do you know about home DNA kits?"

Not much. But, "I've heard they take at least four weeks."

"Ellie's wedding is in a month, so we can't wait that long. The longer the man hangs around Trinity Lakes the more chance there is that people will find out. Ellie is freaking out too. She does not want to feel obliged to have him at her wedding."

Poor Ellie. Jess should be a good friend and bridesmaid and call her. "She doesn't have to invite him."

"Can you imagine what people would say if she didn't?"

People like the Rhonda Ingalls and other gossips of this world. "I didn't think you Reillys cared about the busybodies."

"I don't, but this is Ellie, and she'd really rather not have something like this distract her. She's already too busy as it is."

Right, she was definitely going to call her after this. "What do they do on those TV crime shows?"

He sighed. "Are you suggesting we invite him back for a glass of water or to fingerprint him or something?"

"Fingerprinting is probably not a bad idea. You'd probably get a far quicker result than waiting on a lab to analyze a DNA sample."

"Oh, okay. And who would check that?"

"Sheriff Thompson would know someone."

"We're not involving the law."

She winced. "But if you don't, then things are likely not to go well for you. I'm pretty sure that any evidence you find would be classified as non-legal, which is why I'll keep at you until the cows come home to involve Sheriff Thompson ."

"Please, Jess? Tell me there's another way. If we know there's a chance he's not real then we can rest easier. Mom has barely left her bed since finding out."

Her heart panged. How well she remembered the days when Beth Reilly had been so worn down she'd spent most of the day in bed. It seemed cruel that she'd recovered only to have something like this happen.

But still, one important question remained. "But what if we did find out that it is him?"

He groaned. "Then I guess we'll cross that bridge when we come to it. But we won't know unless we know, right?"

Right. "Okay, I'll see what I can do. But no promises, okay?"

"You're the best."

"You know it."

The call ended, and she sat staring at the phone. Her mind whirled with the overwhelming conflict. Was this man really Cooper's father? If so… Her hands clenched. How dare he treat his children, his wife, in such a way? He deserved to be exposed. And maybe it was sinful of her, but she really didn't want him to be the real Donald Reilly.

COOPER SHOWED UP ON THURSDAY.

She opened the door and her heart hitched at the shadows in his face. "Oh, Coop."

"Jess."

"Come here." She opened her arms and hugged him, and they stayed in each other's arms for a long, long moment. She savored the nearness, his warmth, the rasp of his chin against her cheek.

"I can't be at home anymore, I needed to get out. So I figured

I'd offer my services as your chauffeur today. I brought Mom's car again."

She drew back, peeked over his shoulder. Sure enough his mom's 4X4 sat waiting. She touched his bristled cheek. "Hey, you don't have to do that. I canceled all today's appointments, and—"

"I need to fill my mind with something other than whether this Donald Reilly is our you-know-what." He grimaced. "Please, help me take my mind off it?"

She swallowed, as his gaze dipped to her lips then back. Yes, she could think of other ways to distract him, none of which would be very helpful for either of them right now. "Well, in that case, I'm sure there would be a number of very happy farmers if we visited again."

The rest of the day proved mostly distracting, as he made phone calls and as expected, met with affirmatives for her to visit after all. Cooper drove her to various farms and ranches, carried her bag as she conducted health checks, held horse's hooves as she examined them for foot rot, soothed farmers as she checked on pregnant cows. She hoped it was helping, was getting his mind out of the never-ending cycle of 'what if.' There were too many uncertainties in this world, and the peace that came from trusting in God seemed far away.

Which reminded her. "Hey Coop, can you please pull over here?"

He glanced across. "Here?"

She nodded. He steered onto the verge and she gripped his hand.

"Jess?"

"Close your eyes." She needed to close hers. She didn't want to get distracted by him. "Hey God, thank You that You are with us. Thank You that You know exactly who this man is. If he's Donald, then please reveal that to us. If he's an imposter, then expose him. But give Coop and Beth and Ellie and all the others peace. Help us to trust You. Amen."

———

"AMEN," Cooper echoed. He coughed to clear the emotion clogging his throat. "Thanks."

"Any time." She smiled, and he found an answering one.

This woman. Oh, how he loved this woman. And while so many things remained unsure, he was growing more certain every day that he needed Jess Martin in his life. She was like balm, reminding him of what was truly important. Like God's plans. God's promises. For his family and for the future. For their future? He sure hoped she could see a future with him.

Because this, spending time with Jess, being out on the ranges and ridges, breathing too-fresh air, was exactly what he needed. Being out, doing some hard physical labor—well, hard for a body more used to a desk and ergonomic chair—seeing the way Jess interacted with people older than her, proving her value to the local farming community.

"You're so good at that," he said, as they drove home from the Galbraith ranch.

"Good at what?"

"Listening to people, making them feel heard."

She half-smiled. "I'm just doing my job."

"You do it well."

She turned to face him then. "Can you see why I love being part of the community, and why I want to keep doing this?"

He nodded. "Do you enjoy doing the larger animals or the domestic ones?"

"You know, I was thinking about this the other day, after you said I should consider getting a partner. I think I do prefer the farm visits to all the drama of people's cats and dogs."

"So you'd do the rural visits and the partner could focus on more domestic animals."

"I'd have to help at first, but I think it would be a good way to go. It's something I'm going to talk over with Dad when he returns from their cruise."

Dad. Just the word made his spirits dip again.

"Hey, seeing we're almost at Trinity Lakes, do you mind if we stop at Joe's Diner? I don't know what your plans are for dinner, but I'm starving."

"You're always starving," he said affectionately.

"And I might even be persuaded to pay for my best employee's meal, seeing he's been so good as to drive me around today."

"You might, huh?" He steered to find a parking spot on Main. He found one near the Art Deco-inspired cinema. The movie theater's pistachio green curved walls and rounded windows added an unexpected flair to the street. He glanced at what old movie was showing this week. Maybe a couple of hours watching a cinematic classic would help provide further distraction. And if it meant sitting in the dark next to Jess, all the better.

They moved across the street and he held the door open as they entered Joe's. At once the scent of frying onions and the walls soaked in decades of cooking and love drew a tug in his stomach.

"Someone's hungry, huh?" Jess glanced at him, then Marlene as the waitress directed them to an empty booth.

He ordered a Trinity burger and she got a loaded dog with slaw on the side and an extra serving of fries. Their drinks were ordered, and he spent the time looking around at who else was here. Then froze.

"What is it?"

He lowered his gaze. "Over there. Two o'clock."

She peered behind her. "The old man sitting by himself?"

"That's him," he hissed.

"Him? Oh!" Her eyes widened. "Wow." She swiveled back to face him. "Did you know he was still around?"

"Nope. But I guess we shouldn't be surprised. Why would he show up unannounced then disappear just because we asked him to?"

"If he isn't your father, then why do you think he's doing this?"

"If?" He raised his brows.

"Look, I don't think he could be the real deal either, which is again why I think it's important to mention it to the sheriff—"

She broke off as Marlene placed their chocolate shakes on the table.

"Do you think she heard?" he asked in an undertone.

"I don't know. But the longer you keep this a secret the more chance it has of coming out. And quite possibly in a big way."

He sighed.

She reached across the table and held his hands. "Don't you think you'd be better off dropping a few hints in case he's here for nefarious purposes?"

He almost-smiled. "Nefarious purposes?"

"Look, I might've been reading an old book the other day and the phrase stuck."

"You had time to read a book? Is the sky falling?"

"You mock, but I've already told you about this. You told me to make time for self-care, and I did. I've still got a long way to go, but I'm trying to do better. You were right, and I was wrong, so thank you for pointing it out."

She paid attention to what he said. Admitted when she was wrong. Was appreciative for his advice. They might still have their moments of challenge, but if they weren't in public, he'd admit his feelings once and for all.

"Pray, and then let's change the subject," she said, after thanking Marlene as she deposited the meals on the table.

He held her hand and thanked God for their food, then dug in. Delicious as ever.

"So, I want to know, what is happening with your work? I mean, it's fun having a cute chauffeur and office man, but I'm sure this isn't what you're wanting to do forever."

He placed his burger back on the plate and dabbed at his mouth with the paper napkin. "I've applied for a few jobs."

"And when do you expect to hear back?"

"Soon," he hedged. The email from London still sat unanswered. But how could he answer it when he didn't know what his future was? And now, with his unlikely-but-still-possible father sitting fifteen feet away everything felt even more complicated. He wasn't worried about money—which is why he'd make sure he'd pay for tonight's meal before Jess could— and he could afford to find the right kind of work to suit his interests. But he felt like he was skating close to a lie if he didn't admit to the job offer from London.

That, combined with the lack of honesty about Dream Match and knowing who she was, made him wonder again what she'd say when she found out.

She excused herself to use the bathroom, and he continued to mull things over. His phone buzzed with a notification from Dream Match. He tapped it open. "You have a message waiting."

He opened it. Guilt gnawed. Exactly how was he going to admit to being Jess's dream match? It was kind of awesome how they matched up on the app as well as in real life, but how would she respond if he admitted he knew it was her? She'd never liked surprises.

He glanced across at where the man-who-claimed-to-be-his-father was sitting. His stomach heaved. He hated how this man—*that* man—had caused so much upheaval for his family.

"Donald" pushed his plate away, signaled Marlene for the check, and Cooper was torn between the desire to hide or to get up and follow him. Instead, he propped his head in his hands, half covering his face, as he studied his phone, and prayed that the man wouldn't recognize him and stop to talk—to harangue —about his baseless claims. They had to be baseless, right? He didn't dare contemplate what it would mean if he was proved to be who he said he was.

He peeked through splayed fingers, saw Donald slip some bills to Marlene, then heft to his feet. Behind him, Jess waited, glancing at Marlene, then at the man, then at the table. Cooper resumed hiding his face, pretending to examine his phone, as "Donald" lumbered past, then grew conscious of a person drawing close. Who?

"Here."

He glanced up.

Jess smiled and carefully deposited a fork on top of a fresh napkin. "Let's see if that can get the evidence you need."

"Is this—?"

She nodded, resuming her seat at the table. "I sneaked it. Don't worry, I'll make sure Marlene's tip more than covers the cost of a new fork."

"You think a fork will hold enough DNA?"

"Maybe. It sure beats trying to go covert ops and sneaking a toothbrush. But you gotta start somewhere, right? And we won't know unless we try."

We.

He loved that word. Wanted it to be true again. Soon. He exhaled shakily. "I hate how that man wrecked our lives."

She grasped his hand. "Your life is hardly wrecked, Cooper. You have an awesome family, you've got a great career—"

"Had a great career."

"It's hardly over, Coop. Just on pause for a refresh, right?"

Right. And Jess Martin was his refresh in so many ways. But how could he pursue a relationship with her here and still go forward with his career? "You didn't mention awesome friends."

"That's because I've never been one to toot my own horn."

He smiled. "You should." He pointed to the fork. "That might well save the day."

"I hope so."

"Here you go, hon." Marlene deposited a plastic to-go box on the table. "Although I don't see what leftovers it is you wanted to pack away."

Jess carefully lifted the fork with a paper napkin. "I hope you don't mind if I borrow this. It's for a science experiment."

"You kids with your science learning." Marlene waved a hand. "Go on. We won't miss it. Knives on the other hand…" She winked and moved to the next table.

"So what will you do?" he asked Jess.

"I'll talk to my friend at the lab and see if there's enough sample to test."

"And if there is?"

"Then I hope we'll have an answer soon."

He exhaled. "I don't know what I'd do without you."

"Go back to California?"

Ouch. But he deserved that. "I don't want to go where you're not," he answered honestly.

Her eyes widened. "Cooper."

"Hey, sorry to interrupt you two folks again," Marlene said, "but I just remembered. That guy who was here before, sitting over there?" She pointed to where "Donald" had been sitting there. "It was the strangest thing. I asked him what he was doing in Trinity Lakes and he said he was catching up with long lost family."

His mouth dried. Oh no.

"And you know whose family he said it was?" Marlene eyed Cooper.

He had a bad feeling about this.

"Yours."

CHAPTER ELEVEN

The next day passed in prayers and busyness. Jess sent off the fork to her friend Miranda who worked in a lab and could expedite matters. She had even taken Cooper's advice and sent an email to her dad, knowing it wasn't ideal for him to have to think about this while on vacation, but also knowing that her father needed time before coming around to an idea. If he had time to work out some of the pros and cons before returning to Trinity Lakes then he might be more open to the idea on his return. In one week.

Cooper worked for her Friday, and they were both glad when six pm came and she could shift the sign to say 'closed'. It was funny, but with him around she felt more settled, and more inclined to keep those personal boundaries that helped her feel sane. Cooper was good for her, and it was easy to slip into the old ways of friendship. But it was also weird, in that she wanted more but still felt hamstrung by his lack of clarity around his future—and that little thing called Dream Match. It meant that she wasn't ready to wholly invest in resuming a relationship where once she'd been so happy.

"So, got any plans with Hero Fireman tonight?" Cooper asked.

"Nope. Just a quiet night for me."

His head tilted. "How quiet do you want it?"

"Why?" She smiled. "Do you want to go on a toothbrush scavenger hunt?"

"Not really, no. But I thought it would be nice to go out."

"Two nights in a row? Whoa. Super Cooper is owning the town, huh?"

His lips flicked up on one side. "I haven't heard that phrase for a while."

There was a reason for that. She was the only one who had ever called him that, and he hadn't been super for a while. But these days she was prepared to amend that.

"Anyway, what do you think about celebrating the end of the working week by going to watch a movie with me?"

Her heart hurried faster. Did he mean this to sound like a date? "It might depend on the movie. What's playing?"

"In Trinity Lakes?" He flicked open his phone and read aloud, "*Rear Window*."

"Ooh, you know how to get a girl's interest, don't you?"

"I hope so."

The low raspy tone, and the way he looked at her intently, made her wonder whether he really did intend to resume their relationship. Maybe this could work.

"I don't think you can say something quite like that unless you really intend to see it through," she said.

He shrugged. "It's just a movie."

"Is it?"

His smile kicked her chest, and air was suddenly hard to find. "That's up to you, Jess."

Oh, she hated non-clarification like this. He seemed to be holding all the cards while she was floating along behind wondering what was really real. How could a future work if she was here and he was elsewhere? She was one of those people for whom long distance relationships couldn't work. She barely kept in contact with those she'd gone to college with due to the nature of her work and her tiredness every day. Situational relationships, when she regularly saw the people she interacted with, were so much better. Even trying to pursue BizC on Dream Match was proving how much she'd failed at keeping in contact.

"I don't think you should say things like that," she whispered.

"Say things like what?" He leaned against the kitchen cupboard. "I thought I was being clear. I'd like to see if we can go back to where we were a year ago."

A shaky breath released. "Being good friends?"

"Being more than good friends." His mouth curved again. Oh, she'd missed his mouth on hers. "So what do you say?"

She felt lightheaded. "I'd say yes to the movie, and I need to think about the other."

"Take all the time you need. But the movie starts in twenty so we probably need to hurry."

Twenty-five minutes later she was sitting in the movie theatre with Cooper's arm right next to hers. She felt the sparks of his skin next to hers, so much that she could barely pay attention to the movie, which didn't matter, as she'd seen it before. Trinity Lakes cinema only showed old movies, which was part of the charm of the place. People wanting to see blockbusters and new releases had to go further afield, like Walla Walla.

Cooper's hand laid tantalizingly close to hers. And while she had held his hand numbers of times, even last night, it was different to intentionally holding his hand in the dark like this. With all that he'd said before. With all that had gone before. With all of their history and hopes and friendship and future and… everything.

Before she could think anything more, Cooper's fingers tangled with hers then clasped her palm. She sank deeper into her seat, as Grace Kelly scolded James Stewart on screen, and glanced across at Cooper.

He was watching her, not the screen. He smiled.

"What?" she whispered.

"You remind me of her," he said, pointing to the screen, where the little housekeeper, played by Thelma Ritter, had come on.

"Sarcastic and rolling my eyes?"

"The person who brightens my day."

Oh, he meant Grace Kelly. There probably wasn't a woman alive who wouldn't love to be compared to that beautiful woman. She leaned close, conscious the cinema had other patrons, and murmured, "I remember in this film that he didn't fully appreciate Grace until near the end."

"I think you might've forgotten that he took a lot of things for granted, and didn't realize how much he loved her until he thought he'd lost her."

Her breath caught. Had Cooper meant to imply that he loved her? She pivoted to watch the screen, but even though she'd watched the film five times before, the story was a blur. She couldn't pay attention, not when his thumb caressed her wrist, sending her insides to a frenzy.

She barely noticed the film except by the way his grip tightened during the scenes when Grace was in the apartment of the suspected murderer. Cooper had watched this film before too, but they never watched it like this, holding hands, their future holding as many unknowns as the intruder in the apartment opposite James Stewart.

As the movie drew closer to the end, she wondered what this would mean for the two of them. Was he declaring his intentions toward her? Or was this just more of what had happened in the past, where he'd kissed her, then killed their relationship in front of the all-too-observant neighbors of Trinity Lakes? She really didn't want to go down that same route again.

The movie reached its dramatic climax, then there came a loud sigh of relief behind them, as the final scenes played out and then the credits rolled.

"I love that movie," she said, as the room's light turned back up to dim.

"I know." He squeezed her hand.

She smiled at him, then noticed a man moving. No. Was that Donald?

She touched Cooper's cheek, drawing his face closer to her, to avoid the man seeing him.

"What is it?" Cooper asked.

"Donald," she mouthed.

"Where?"

"Behind you."

His eyebrows arched, then he leaned forward, and whispered, "Sorry, but I'm not sorry about this."

His breath skimmed her lips, then he kissed her.

The shock of his lips on hers lasted but a second before memories flared. His kiss was soft and hesitant, then hungry and full, igniting her into passion. Her hand tangled in his curls as she tugged him closer. She soon lost herself in the kiss, not caring that others were nearby, not caring about what anyone else might think. Cooper was hers, and she was his, and this was how things were always meant to be. And sure, there might be some complications about the future and a whole lot of unknowns, but in this moment everything was right.

After a long, beautiful, thorough moment he pulled back and sighed. "I'd forgotten how much I love kissing you."

"I hadn't."

He grinned. "That I love kissing you?"

The other, but this worked too. "You know you just made a public statement, don't you?"

"I hope so. I've been looking for an excuse to do that for a while now."

He had? So it wasn't just about hiding from his mystery man father? Oh, he was taking this more seriously than she'd dared hope. "I hope you mean that, because it's going to be all over Trinity Lakes tomorrow. I'm pretty sure I saw Rhonda Ingalls over there."

"Good. The sooner that Fireman Stan knows you're out of bounds the better."

"Are you jealous?"

"Not my proudest moment, but yeah."

"You know there was never any reason to be jealous of him."

"From where I was standing there seemed to be plenty of reasons to be jealous."

Her heart sang. "You know he only came to help with my fire."

"Well, if you have any other problem, I want you to call me."

"That was pretty hard when you were in California."

"But I'm not now. I'm here." He picked up their clasped hands and kissed hers. "With you."

Her skin danced at his touch, but his statement stomped on her hopes. She had to ask. "But for how long?"

His lips pressed together, his eyes growing serious. He rubbed a loose strand of her hair. "That is the question. I'm going to make some more local inquiries and see what I can discover."

"I can't leave Trinity Lakes, you know that, don't you?"

"And I'm not asking you to. I want a future with you, Jess, and I will do what I can to make it happen."

She nodded, even as a little voice inside said she'd heard similar things before.

But maybe this time would be different. *Please Lord.*

He meant it before. He loved kissing Jess. It seemed her lips were made for his and his for her. Part of him still couldn't believe that she'd embraced the opportunity as much as he had. But every part of him was glad she had. And he truly didn't mind that it was in public. Going public made him accountable for his actions, knowing that what he did would affect her reputation. It meant he had to treat her honorably, and just like she'd requested, with intent for their future.

But kissing her also demonstrated to the Trinity Lakes community that their vet was more than just someone who was needed in times of crisis for the animals, but someone who deserved a life of her own. And the way he was feeling now, buzzing like a million bees had taken up residence within, he could totally see a future with her. If only God would let him see how that future could unfold.

He said as much to his mom the next day, as they gathered waiting for the family video call. Jackson was outside in the barn, dealing with another new calf, Lexi was at work, and the house was quiet.

"And you think she reciprocates those feelings?" his mom asked.

Judging from Jess's kiss she surely did. "I get that impression."

Her eyes lit as she smiled. "You two are meant to be together. I'm so glad you've figured that out at last."

"I've known it forever, Mom. Just had a few stumbles along the way."

"So what does it mean for your job?"

"That's the million-dollar question. I've had a job offer from London, but I can't take that." He needed to let them know. "I could probably get something in Seattle, but even that feels too far away."

"I know it hasn't been as easy as Ellie thought it might be, being away from Jasper as much as she is. I think that has contributed to their decision to get married soon."

"I think we could definitely make long distance work, or at least a situation where I'm here most of the time, but fly occasionally. I need you to pray that I don't mess it up again."

"I'll be praying, son."

"Mess what up?" Jackson said as he entered the office where the computer was set up.

"Nothing." Cooper had zero interest in discussing his love life with his brother.

"Let me guess: Doc Martin." Jackson smirked.

How did he always do that? Was Cooper that obvious? Maybe Jess's ability to wear her heart on her sleeve was contagious. He clamped his lips shut.

Fortunately, the computer dinged with the notification that Ellie, Dermott, and Mitchell were ready. So, after greeting their mom, the family conference began.

"So, what's the latest?" Mitchell demanded.

"Jess has sent a specimen to her friend in the lab and asked her to compare it to a sample from me," Cooper said. "She said we should know about the DNA in the next day or so."

"I heard people can do it in hours," Mitchell complained.

"If they're police labs. You didn't want to do that, remember?"

Dermott sighed. "I kind of wish I could see him, and talk to him."

"Why?" Ellie asked, frowning.

"So I could figure out if he's anything like the man I barely remember."

"Well, you can't talk to him," Cooper said, "but I do have a couple of pictures." He posted the photos onto their chat, thanking God that Jess had possessed the foresight to take them the other day.

"Huh. He looks so weedy. Nothing like what I remember," Dermott said.

"Yeah." Mitchell squinted at the screen. "I know it's been years, but he's nothing like that man I hate to remember."

"But is that the problem?" Cooper hated to be the devil's advocate, but it needed to be said. "What if we're all not wanting him to be Donald because of what he's done? What if he really is our father? What do we do then?"

"Ignore him," said Ellie. "Like he has us these past hundred years. I'm not having him at my wedding."

"Nobody is saying you need to," Jackson soothed.

"Good, because I'm not."

Cooper didn't want to point out the intricacies of having a wedding in a public space like a church and whether a member of the public could be kicked out if that was the case.

"I don't think it's fair to Mom if he does hang around," Mitchell said. "This has got to be eating you up, Mom."

"I'm okay now," their mother murmured. "Just trying to trust the Lord."

"Amen." Cooper patted her back.

"But what do we do if he *is* him? Do we have a legal right to keep him away?" Ellie said.

Mitchell sighed. "I spoke to a lawyer yesterday—"

"What? So someone else knows?" Dermott asked. "It's bad enough Coop had to go telling Jessica—"

"She's trustworthy," Cooper insisted. "And she's helping us out, remember?"

"Come on, Dermott," Ellie rolled her eyes. "She's practically family, anyway. You know it's only a matter of time until she is."

Whoa, Ellie. "You need to calm that farm on down."

Jackson snickered. "I love how Coop moves back to the ranch then starts pulling out all these farming clichés."

Cooper rolled his eyes. Whatever.

"Nobody else knows any specifics," Mitchell assured. "I was

just talking hypotheticals about what happens if someone is legally declared dead. I'm afraid it could turn into a huge mess, which is why we need this DNA sample to come back negative."

No joke.

The siblings' discussion went to and fro until Cooper noticed his mom was very still. "Mom, are you okay?"

His mother sighed. "I just can't get over all the things he knows about us. He wouldn't have known those things unless he was Donald."

"Unless Donald told him," Jackson said.

"But why would he then come here?" Ellie asked.

"Yeah." Jackson's brow puckered. "And while Mitchell and Cooper might be doing okay financially, it's not as if the ranch is rolling in cash. It's not like this is land with oil or gold or where there is a great fortune to be discovered."

The ranch was rolling better financially these days, thanks to Cooper's savvy tips and Liam Darcy's rental of fields for his solar project, but Jackson was right. These fields weren't paved with gold.

"And that's why I can't help but wonder if he is your father after all," their mom said. "He's got nothing to benefit from coming here except us."

"What is your gut telling you about this, Mom?" Ellie asked.

Mom closed her eyes, and Cooper placed a hand on her back and prayed for her. If it was this confusing for him it must be so hard for her.

"I don't think he is," she whispered.

Mitchell crossed his arms and nodded. "I think he's an imposter too."

"I think we all think that," Jackson said.

"We all hope that anyway," Cooper pointed out. "But you know that it's important that we're all on the same page about this. That's why we're having this meeting today."

"Speaking of, I need to get to the pre-skate soon," Mitchell said.

"Where are you today?" Dermott asked.

"In Toronto. Playing Dan Walton and his crew."

"Good luck," Jackson said.

"Yeah, we'll need it. Toronto's been on fire lately."

"Before you go, I think we should pray about this," Cooper said.

"Well, go you." Ellie grinned. "And I mean, go you. Go for it, Coop. Pray for us."

So he closed his eyes to avoid his brothers' wide-eyed shocked stares. "Hey God, we really need Your help with this situation. You see the truth of it. You know whether this man is who he is claiming to be, or if he is an impostor. If he's an impostor then we pray that You would help us expose that and reveal his motives. If he is the real deal, then show us what to do next. Thank You that You are with us and we can trust You, and bless this family and especially Mom. Amen."

"Amen."

"Good prayer, bro." Ellie smiled.

"Thank you, Cooper." Mom gave him a side-hug.

Mitchell made his farewell and his square dissolved from the video chat, leaving the rest of them to catch up. Jackson asked about Dermott's family, and he shared about Mindy and the kids. "But you'll see them soon at Ellie's wedding."

"I can't believe it's coming so soon," Ellie said. "I'm so glad we're not waiting forever to get married. What's the point? Especially when you know the person so well, and well, yeah."

"And when you want to get on with making babies, right?" Jackson said.

"Jackson!" Ellie said. "I have no desire for a baby just yet."

"Don't say stuff like that in front of your mother," Dermott reproved.

"I'm pretty sure she understands."

"I can speak for myself, thank you, boys. And yes, I think it's a good thing that Ellie and Jasper aren't waiting around. Especially when they've known each other for so long."

Like Cooper and Jess had. He'd known her even longer than Ellie had known Jasper. And while they might not have been best friends forever, they'd been friends long enough for him to know he'd found his forever girl.

His heart hitched.

"Yo, Coop. Why are you looking like that?" Dermott asked.

This face-revealing-his-feelings thing was getting way too old.

"Are you thinking about your perfect match, huh?" Ellie teased.

Her words reminded him he needed to deal with the Dream Match situation. To tell Jess the truth. He could've done it last night, but he hadn't wanted to spoil the evening with that particular truth-bomb. And this afternoon she'd gone car buying, before a party tonight with a few of the young women from church.

He'd try to speak to her about it tomorrow. And pray that the DNA result would come back soon.

"Don't forget, we'll have another family meeting when we know we have a result," he said instead.

Now he just needed to see what would happen next.

And whether Jess could find her dream match in him.

CHAPTER TWELVE

"And I can't believe we're back here again, but little Flossie seems to be having pain, is always dragging her butt on the ground, scooting along like she's got worms. But I'm sure she can't have them because I've been giving her the worming tablets like you said."

"Poor thing." Jess rubbed the terrier's ears. "She probably just needs to get her glands expressed again."

"Would you mind?"

"Not at all. I'll do that now, if you'd like to wait outside."

"Yes, ma'am."

Jess did the deed—joy, but something the dog, and its owner, would appreciate—and took the pup back to the room where Mrs. Brookes waited.

"Oh, Flossie. You look so much happier now."

Jess might be the vet but she couldn't see any noticeable difference in the dog's demeanor. But okay. "If you could please take Flossie outside, Cooper will be able to fix you up."

"How long until your parents return?"

"They'll be back at the end of the week."

And she'd have to say goodbye to her special handsome helper.

She smiled and held the door open as Mrs. Brookes and Flossie exited, her gaze lifting to Coop, who eyed her with a smile of his own. There had been some comments about their kiss at the movies when she caught up with the girls on Saturday night.

"That's a big weekend for you, with a new car and a new man," Elissa Darcy had said.

"A secondhand car," she'd mumbled. Goodbye Big Red. And hello, Big Blue. The pre-owned Suburban was a good buy, Brandon had assured, and she already loved it.

"And a second chance at romance?" Lexi had asked.

She'd blushed, not knowing what to say, even though it felt pretty true. There had been more comments and smiling looks when she'd sat next to Cooper at church yesterday. And while she'd never liked being the cause for speculation, the fact that people seemed kindly interested rather than merely gossiping made things better.

That, and the fact that yesterday after church she and Cooper had managed a picnic together by the lake, thanks to the milder weather. It was such a funny time of year with the varying temperatures. But taking time out to lie on a picnic blanket and gaze up at the blue sky and close her eyes had been the perfect way to relax after another busy week. Cooper was good for her. Making her stop and smell the roses and do the things that she wouldn't do on her own. Holding hands with him while they accepted the gentle kiss of the sun had been a perfect day to escape the pressures and those questions that had arisen during the week. And the questions that hung over the future still.

Miranda, her lab friend, had assured her that the DNA sample should have a result today. And she was trying to give her full attention to each patient. But it was tricky when all she wanted to do was call Miranda to find out the result. Cooper was proving to be far more patient, and she was grateful for that. He might not have been the most patient person in the past, but the fact he could be patient now proved they could be a good partnership.

She glanced at the list of her next appointments. Suppressed a sigh. She'd prefer to never deal with Mrs. Jansson again, but unfortunately poor Dolly couldn't pay the price of her owner's rudeness. "Dolly?"

Before Mrs. Jansson went in, Cooper drew her aside. "Just checking you have means to pay today, ma'am."

Mrs. Jansson gasped. "I can't believe you would ask me that!"

The other patrons glanced at her now, her gasp drawing attention in a way that Cooper's soft question hadn't done. Jess swallowed a smile, appreciating his efforts.

Mrs. Jansson was much meeker than their last encounter, and barely even complained when Jess's phone rang during the visit.

Jess glanced at the screen. Miranda. "Excuse me, I need to take this."

"But—"

"I said, I need to take this." She moved to the room beyond. "Miranda? Do you have an answer? If so, don't tell me what the answer is, just let me know if the sample had enough on it to be helpful."

"Helpful?" Miranda laughed.

Oh no. If waiting for a few days was this hard, how much more difficult would it be if they had to go through this process again? It would've been a lot simpler to get the police involved.

"It was exactly what we needed, so yes, there is a result."

"Thank You Jesus," she prayed aloud.

"Amen," Miranda said. "Look, I get that this wasn't for you but for a 'friend,' so I won't tell you what it is, but I'll email it to you with a document attached. I hope it's good news for you all."

"Me too. Thanks so much. You're a lifesaver."

"Just remember next time I'm in town you owe me dinner."

"You got it."

She hung up, and moved through the room where Mrs. Jansson waited. "Excuse me. I'll be a moment longer."

She peeked out at the filled waiting room and caught Cooper's eye. His chin tilted and she nodded. He blew out a breath, and mouthed a "thanks."

An email notification showed that Miranda had sent it through, so she forwarded him the email as she had promised earlier, along with her offer to pray.

Yesterday he had said something about not wanting to open it until he was with the rest of his family, and she was certain he was going to try and meet with his family this afternoon while she was busy. And while she understood the need for urgency, she was also a little disappointed that she wouldn't be part of that conversation. But Cooper had said he would like her to join them for dinner tonight, so she hoped that tonight might provide the answers they needed.

She refocused on Dolly, but for the rest of the afternoon her heart was with the Reilly family. She snatched every minute she could to pray for them, to pray for their peace, and that whatever the outcome was, they would know God's hand in it all.

She barely dared contemplate what would happen if they were to learn that the man was their dad. Ellie would be devastated, and Jess figured her duties as chief bridesmaid would consist more of consoling the bride-to-be than picking out flowers and wedding favors.

That evening she fed the cats then drove Big Blue to the Reilly ranch. Ellie's vehicle was there too. She knocked on the door then opened it, as in the tradition of many years, and was unsurprised to see Jasper Cohen in the room too.

"Hey." She hugged Ellie. "How did it go?"

"We haven't opened it yet."

"No?"

"We had to wait for Mitchell to finish a game, and while it's super late for him and Dermott, they wanted to do it this way."

"Besides, you're the one who was able to make this happen for us," Cooper said, "and I thought it was only fair to make sure you were in on the action."

"You didn't have to," she protested.

"I wanted to." Cooper smiled.

"We all wanted you to be here," Beth assured. "So, who's going to start the call and do the deed?"

"I'll get the call happening." Ellie tapped on the computer keyboard. "And Mom, I think it's only right that you be the one to find out."

Beth sighed. "I don't think I'm strong enough." She glanced at Cooper, but he shook his head.

"I know it's my blood, but I think Jackson should be the one who finds out first. Especially as he's the one who has power of attorney and has been running the ranch these past years. The buck stops with him, and it will affect him the most if it's proved to be true, so he should do it."

By now the computer screen showed several faces, Dermott and his wife Mindy, and Mitchell, whose damp hair and helmet-marked face said it hadn't been too long since he'd finished his game.

"Hey there." Cooper lifted a hand. "Just letting you know that we've got a few extras here. Jasper and Jess, say hi."

"Hi." Jess waved at the screen.

"This is your doing, huh?" Mitchell asked her.

"My friend Miranda does this kind of thing all the time," she said. "She said it had over 99% accuracy."

He nodded, expression grim. "Thanks. Let's hope she got the right result."

She bit back her response. There was definitely a result, but whether the Reilly family would consider it the right result was something they were about to find out.

"So who is opening it?" Dermott asked.

"I am," Jackson said.

"Here." Cooper shifted the computer mouse and pointed to the screen. "Just press to open there."

"Okay," Jackson said, settling in his seat, Lexi placing a hand on his shoulder. "Here goes."

Jess shifted to watch their expressions. Soon she'd know exactly whether the result was to be considered right or not. She prayed that whatever the result, everyone would remain calm…

Jackson began reading. She knew from other DNA results she'd seen that chromosomes were tested, as the likelihood of parentage was tested against the DNA sequence or alleles in the child. The sheer volume of potential outcomes made DNA matching the gold standard to testing paternity.

"I'm afraid I don't understand what this all says."

"Just read it, Jackson," Mitchell pleaded.

"Fine then. The following conclusion is based on the non-matching alleles observed at the STR loci listed above with a DI equal to zero."

Jess grinned, catching Lexi's eye. She was beaming too.

"You're smiling," Ellie said. "So it's good news?"

Jackson cleared his throat. "The alleged father is therefore excluded as the biological father of the child. The probability of paternity is zero percent."

"Thank you Lord!" Cooper said, hugging his mom then Jess.

The family's celebrations were quickly followed by calls to inform the police. "He's an imposter," Mitchell said. "A con man."

"I can't believe he thought he'd get away with it," Jackson

huffed. "Surely he must've known a DNA test would happen sooner or later."

"I think he underestimated the Reilly family."

Cooper wrapped an arm around Jess. "And their loved ones."

"Loved ones?" she murmured, as everyone hushed.

"Oh, you know you're Cooper's loved one," Ellie said.

"One hundred percent." Cooper bent to kiss her as laughter filled the room.

———

IT WAS funny how something that had felt so enormous, weighing on them so heavily, could be resolved so quickly. Within days of informing Sheriff Thompson about their alleged father's "reappearance," he'd tracked the man down and brought him in for questioning.

Cooper and his siblings and mom had decided not to own up to the DNA test, and the murky ethics of how that had been orchestrated, and were confident a new DNA test would suffice. Not that it was needed. Not when fingerprints revealed "Donald" was really Mark Stoybels, who was quickly detained in custody then shipped back to an Arizona prison where he'd escaped five years ago.

"But how did he know all that stuff about Donald?" Cooper had asked, when the sheriff was able to discuss matters with them.

"Turns out they first met at AA—"

That'd be right.

"—and he gleaned a few things about Donald Reilly. Then, he went to jail, then when he escaped, he found your father." The sheriff glanced at Cooper's mom. "I'm sorry, ma'am, but we found your husband's remains."

Cooper exhaled. "So he really is dead."

Sheriff Thompson nodded. "He really is. The DNA sample matched the one you gave us, so we know that for certain."

"And this Stoybels man killed him?"

"He made a full confession. Yes."

Jackson rubbed his hand over his face. "So are you saying that when we legally had him declared dead, he wasn't?"

"No. But back then, remember nobody could find him, despite their best efforts. And he'd gone interstate and changed his name, although he'd obviously kept some remnants of the past, like his wedding ring. The perp said he found that in a cash box, along with some other documents. But you don't need to worry about the legalities. That was all sorted by the law, so there is nothing to concern yourself with."

"I just want this over," Mom said.

"It is over, Beth," Sheriff Thompson said. "It's finally over."

Hallelujah.

Cooper wasn't sure if some part of him was supposed to be sad, but he couldn't find it in his heart to care. Maybe some might call that unchristian of him, but while Donald Reilly might've contributed to Cooper's DNA, he'd contributed little to his life. Apart from making his mom's life incredibly hard.

But even that experience had taught his family how to be resilient, how to work hard, how to value those they cared about. These were qualities he wouldn't trade for anything. Qualities he wanted to continue in his own family one day. Which meant he really needed to find a local job, and then finally explain a few things to Jess, and see if she'd agree to a future with him.

CHAPTER THIRTEEN

"You're back!"

Jess hugged her parents, heard their news, caught them up.

They were tired after their flight, but after a nap, they were ready to talk about how she'd been coping in their time away.

"You look tired, honey," Mom said.

Truth time. "I have been tired, Mom. And I know that I can't continue this way."

"You mentioned that Cooper has been helping you."

"He was great, a real blessing, but we all know he's not a vet receptionist. Mom, Dad," she looked at them. "We really need to consider our options about the future of Martin's Veterinary Services."

"What are you saying?" her father asked.

"I just can't keep doing things this way, Dad," she said. "I'm not as tough as you or Grandad."

"Nobody ever said you needed to be."

"But the way the practice has grown, with all the new people in Trinity Lakes and surrounds, it is really tough to stay on top of it all." She sighed. "I thought I was tougher than I am, but I've come to realize that I tend to overwork, and I've been exhausted for a really long time."

God bless Cooper for helping her see this.

She faced her father. "And like I said in my email, I really think we need to take on a new partner."

He blew out a breath. "I must admit your email caught me a little by surprise. I know it's not been easy."

"It was much easier when Cooper could help out. But it's unreasonable to expect him to be able to continue, especially when he gets his new job."

"What is his new job?" Mom asked.

"He said he's fine-tuning a few things and that he'd tell me tonight." During their very necessary date. The past few days had been so busy they'd barely had a chance to talk.

"So you two are back together again?" Mom asked.

"Yes," she admitted shyly. "I think we both came to realize that we could've done things differently instead of letting things end the way they did."

"Are you sure about him, honey?"

Jess nodded. "Surer than almost anything." The only thing more sure was that God really did have good things lined up for them. And yes, it might not always be easy, but with Him walking beside them every step of the way, they need not fear or doubt. Just like the Shepherd's Psalm said, though they might walk through the valley of the shadow of death they need fear no evil, for God's rod and staff comforted them, leading and guiding and stopping them from going down the wrong paths. God was with them, and as God continued to be with them, she knew that whatever happened in the future would ultimately work out.

Mom smiled. "I've always liked Cooper."

"I hope you also like what he's done with tweaking the scheduling system," Jess said.

"I know what that young man did before helped us in all

kinds of ways, so I think it will work out just fine. Even though I suspect I might need a little bit of training in understanding it."

"He said it's pretty straightforward."

"He might say it, but I hope he'll be merciful to an older brain that's just spent a glorious amount of time in the Caribbean."

"You can trust him, Mom."

"I know."

"So I suppose we better start considering how we're going to go about getting a partner." Dad frowned.

"Well, we could advertise."

"And pray."

"You never know who's looking for a change of pace to a small-town life."

She hoped Cooper was. Then wondered if that was part of what Cooper wanted to say to her tonight. He'd seemed excited, and after all the drama with his family, perhaps he'd figured out how to get this resolved as well.

"Well, tell me what else has been happening."

Jess filled them in on the Reilly's news, which was met with disbelief. "How could anyone be so cruel to that poor family? Oh, poor Beth."

"I think she's doing okay, all things considered." Part of that might be to do with the fact that she'd seen Beth having tea and scones at the Bellbird café yesterday with Mr. Johnson. "That's what Cooper says, anyway. Oh," she hurried on, to stave off her mother's non-subtle interrogation about Cooper. "And we had a little party for Ellie recently. She's getting excited about her wedding next weekend. I'm glad you're back for it."

"We wouldn't have missed it for the world."

"So the party was fun?"

"Really fun." She'd enjoyed chatting with Hallie and Esther, and Georgia Darcy had come too.

Ellie had teased Georgia about Mitchell, but she'd only blushed and ignored her.

"And what has been happening with you, Jess?" Elissa Darcy had asked.

She'd explained about her recent work and the fact she'd hope they'd get a new partner soon, and a new admin assistant, "because Cooper is awesome, but super overqualified for that role."

"A new job? This is Ellie's brother, right? I think I've heard Liam mention him before."

"He's worked with several big-name companies over the years." She dropped a few names.

Elissa's eyes widened. "I didn't realize he was that smart."

"Anything tech or systems he's the man."

Elissa had nodded, and the evening had continued with all kinds of Ellie Reilly-worthy amusements, which she shared with her mom now.

"I'm glad you had a good time," her mom said. "It's wonderful to see you are taking the chance to have some fun."

Another of Cooper's encouragements. He was so good for her. She hoped he thought she was good for him.

How silly to think she once had thought she'd find her dream guy on Dream Match. Sure, it worked for others, but she'd already met her match.

She winced. Which reminded her. She really needed to put an end to that connection, then delete the app. And possibly never tell Cooper just how close she'd come to meeting a man who might hold a number of similar qualities, but could never quite match up to her own real-life perfect match.

HER FINGER HOVERED over the keys. "Lord, how do I say this?"

Suddenly the words were there. *Hi BizC. Long time, no talk. Sorry.*

Her phone lit up not a minute later. *Hey BlessBess. I've missed you. Is everything okay?*

She sighed. *I think so. But I thought I should let you know I recently reconnected with an old friend.*

BizC: *By 'old friend' you mean former boyfriend?*

Yes. I want to see if we can make a real go of things this time.

BizC: *I understand.*

Oh, he was sweet.

BizC: *How do you know things have changed for it to work out this time?*

Good question. *He seems more committed. I'm hoping he'll stay in my small town rather than go back to the city.*

Long distance is hard, he typed back.

But not impossible. Not if both people are trying to make a real go of things. Like she would.

BizC: *I hope it works out for you.*

Thanks, she replied. *You too.*

Her heart pinched a little—BizC was a nice guy, and she hoped he found his dream match soon—but she didn't want the temptation of this if things got hard with Cooper again. In so many ways he was her perfect match, and she was committed to working things out. So she cancelled her account, then deleted the app.

Weight rolled off her chest and she pushed back her shoulders.

"Okay, Cooper Reilly, I'm all in."

SHE OPENED the door to see Cooper dressed in a suit. Her breath hitched. "Well, hello."

"Hello to you too."

She grasped his outstretched hand then he twirled her under it. Her dress flowed out as it had been designed to do.

He whistled. "Someone decided to outshine all the other ladies in Trinity Lakes tonight."

"You said dress up. I still don't know why."

"I figure there are a few things to celebrate."

Her pulse increased. Did that mean he did have news about a job?

He drove to the Country Club, and they were escorted to a more private corner of the restaurant. The space was quiet, with candles on the tables like she imagined at those restaurants from Valentine's Day. That day felt so long ago now.

"You approve?" he asked.

"It's beautiful."

His eyes didn't leave her face. "Sure is."

Her cheeks heated. Oh, he was sweet. But the sense she needed to confess about her online dating app only grew.

Guilt made it hard to swallow the sourdough bread and olive oil starter.

"Are you having trouble there?" His forehead pleated. "If you don't want to stay…"

"No, I want to. It's just I needed to say something."

"Something like… how handsome I am?"

She chuckled. "Well, it certainly won't be about how modest you are."

He grinned, snagged her hand. "You're funny."

"You're sweet."

"You're right."

Miss Right? The question burned on her tongue.

But something else burned on her heart. She drew her hand away. "Um, I need to confess something."

———

COOPER'S HEART KICKED. She wasn't the only one. Still, he'd do the gentlemanly thing and let her go first. "What is it?"

She sighed. "Remember last year when we split up?"

"I really don't want to." He clasped her hand again. Her palm was sweaty.

"Well, anyway, after we broke up, I joined a dating app, and—"

"Hey, I don't need to know."

"But I'm just trying to be honest."

"I know. I appreciate that, BlessBess. Your honesty is one of the qualities I like most about you."

Her eyes widened. "What did you say?"

"I really like the fact you're honest?"

"No." She pulled her hand away. "What did you call me?"

"Jess?"

"No, you said something else." She frowned. "Have you been on my phone?"

Okay, this little joke wasn't tracking as he'd thought. "I've been too busy," he enunciated that word slowly, "to jump on your phone. Not that I would, because that would be an invasion of privacy, right?"

"Right. Huh." Her shoulders dropped. "I could've sworn I heard you say—"

"I was BizC."

"Yeah, I know."

No, she didn't.

She sighed. "Anyway, apparently this man I connected with was too busy as well, which turned out for the best really, because you were back, and we were starting to reconnect, and anyway, I thought you should know I deleted the app."

"You deleted it?" Man. He should've done that too. The only reason he hadn't was in case she'd messaged him again. But after that last goodbye message, he should've realized… "I'm glad."

She winced. "I really wasn't sure whether to tell you, but I didn't want to have secrets. Anyway, now you know."

And she still didn't. "You've been a popular lady."

"What do you mean?"

"Well, between your fireman—"

She rolled her eyes.

"—and your Dream Match dude, and me—"

"Did you say Dream Match?" Her brow puckered. "How did you know? You did see my phone, didn't you?"

"No. As I said, I was BizC."

Her head tilted.

"Biz C," he said it more slowly. "And you're Bless Bess."

She blinked. "What?"

"Bless Bess. That's you, isn't it? On Dream Match."

Her mouth sagged. "You're Biz C?"

"Business-focused Cooper. Who's busy." He smiled. "I thought I was being cute with the pun but maybe not. Anyway, apparently you're my dream match."

"I can't believe this." Her eyes were so wide. "How long have you known?"

"A week? Two?"

"You're really my dream match?"

"I hope so."

He watched her as she seemed to waver between hurt and confusion, then she stood.

He rose too. "Jess?"

She took a step toward him then flung herself at him. "Of *course* you're my dream match. You've always been the right man for me."

He wrapped his arms around her waist and tugged her close. Then kissed her. This kiss held both assurance and a promise for the future.

"I can't believe I didn't know," she murmured against his chest a short time later.

"You've been a little busy lately, too."

She laughed, tilting back her head, and he pressed a kiss to her throat.

"Ahem."

He glanced behind them to where a snooty Country Club patron was staring with scandalized eyes. Hmm. Seemed romantic exuberance was frowned upon here.

"Looks like our meals are on their way," Jess murmured, as a waitress neared.

"Looks like we'll have to enjoy more dessert later."

Her eyes sparkled. "I'm always ready for dessert."

He laughed, they sat, ate, and he spilled his own secret.

"So, you know how I've been praying for a job?"

She nodded. "I've been praying too."

He kissed her knuckles. "Well, two days ago I got a phone call from someone who has offered me a role."

Her brow creased. "Is it in the US?"

He nodded.

"Is it on the west coast?"

"Yep."

"Are we really playing games?"

"Yes."

She laughed. "Okay, is it local-ish?"

"Pretty local."

"How local?"

"Is Trinity Lakes local enough for you?"

She gasped. "No way."

"Way."

"Are you serious?"

"One hundred percent." He smiled and told her about Liam Darcy's job offer, helping his various green businesses with the development of apps and other aspects of technology. "It means I can work remotely but also will need to accompany him occasionally on some of his big trips around North America, and potentially the world."

"Oh my goodness! That sounds incredible."

He nodded. "I know. It seemed as random as anything, but

he told me that he's had his eye on me for a while, but it just hadn't been the right timing until now." He smiled. "Apparently somebody said something to his wife recently about me needing a new job, and he figured it was the right time to reach out."

Her eyes widened. "Really?"

"I gathered from what he said that you might know the person responsible. I think she deserves a big kiss as a thank you."

Her lips tilted. "She probably does."

"Apparently that someone is extremely beautiful, and compassionate, and—oh, did I mention?—has exceptional taste in men."

"You did not mention that, no."

"Well, apparently this extremely beautiful and compassionate woman has exceptional taste in—"

"Okay, okay, I might've mentioned something to Elissa recently. I certainly didn't know it would lead to this."

"I'm really glad it did." He held her hand and gently squeezed it. "You are a real blessing to me, you know that?"

"That's what I want to be. Someone you can rely on, who will always have your best interests at heart."

Her words burrowed close into his heart. "The feeling is entirely mutual. I want you to feel like I'm a blessing to you too."

Naturally, his words demanded he prove how much of a blessing she was to him, so he pressed his lips to her hand again and again until he was fairly sure some members of the Country Club were a little startled. But he wasn't going to let stuffy people's opinions affect them.

So what if Mrs. Jansson was looking at them funny. Jess wasn't the vet tonight, she was a woman out on a date with her boyfriend. And it was so nice to have this sense of freedom and feel like they could relax and just be. For the first time in a long time.

"What are you smiling about?" Jess asked him.

He drew his chair closer to hers. "You."

"And why is that?"

"Because I think—no, I'm completely sure about something."

"What's that?"

A rush of something golden filled him, filling his chest with warmth and light, but he knew this was way more than a feeling. It was a certainty, borne of trials, proved through patience, mercy and long-suffering, showed by her generous heart that only inspired him to want to be kind-hearted too.

He tucked a tendril of hair behind her ear. "I wonder if you're thinking the same thing I am, that I've thought for years."

"What's that?" she breathed.

He traced her cheek with his fingertips. "I love you," he murmured. "I always have. And I always will."

"Oh, Coop." She leaned close and whispered against his lips, "I love you too. I suspect I always have, and I know I always will."

"And do you, Jasper Cohen, take Eloise Reilly, to be your wife, to have and to hold, for richer for poorer, for better for worse, in sickness and in health, for as long as you both shall live?"

"I do."

Jess shivered. Her gaze lifted to Cooper's on the other side of the church, and as if he knew she was thinking about him his gaze connected with hers and he smiled.

She grinned back, not caring that half of Trinity Lakes could see them. If they'd seen that recent display in the Country Club restaurant, they'd know she and Cooper were well and truly back together.

In fact, she wondered if today had given him any ideas.

Pastor Ladan continued the ceremony, then Jasper and Ellie kissed, to the congregation's cheers, and Jess and Cooper followed them down the aisle.

Later, they posed for photos outside the Reilly's barn, the barn cleaned up and dressed up for the first time since the New Year's Eve party from a few years ago.

She had vague memories of Liam Darcy meeting Elissa, and that not going well. Proof that even the strongest relationships had their ups and downs.

Her smile deepened as Cooper obeyed the photographer's instruction and inched closer.

"Did I tell you how beautiful you look today?" Cooper murmured.

"I don't believe you did."

"That's funny, because I've been thinking it every second since you first walked through the doors at the church." He kissed her in a breath-stealing moment worthy of its own photo shoot.

"Do you two mind? This is my wedding day," Ellie said.

"Sorry, sis."

"Actually, I don't mind at all," Jess confessed, resulting in a shout of laughter from Jasper.

"Perfect!" the photographer called. "Yes, now that's what we're talking about." She examined her camera screen. "Oh, yes. That one is a keeper."

"You better keep cracking those jokes, Jess," Jasper said.

"It wasn't a joke," Cooper said, wrapping his arm around her and drawing her nearer. "This one means what she says."

"And she says what she means," Ellie said.

And Jess did mean it. She was so happy to be at a place where she felt relieved and free to be able to tell the man she loved how she felt, not caring if others saw or judged her or made comments. Cooper Reilly was a good man, and the fact he loved her, despite her many flaws, made her heart sing. And she didn't mind being focused on him, and she knew that Ellie would understand too.

"Okay, now let's have one with all of you looking serious."

Jess joined the others in striking a pose, staring down the camera like she imagined a movie actress like Ainsley Beckett might do. She peeked at Cooper, who wore his own tilted chin glance, like Lincoln Cash in a movie. So handsome.

"That's great." The photographer pointed to Jess. "Loved how you were checking out your man there."

"I wasn't checking him out."

"You can, you know," Cooper murmured. "You have my full permission, any time."

Their audience—comprising mostly of Cooper's siblings and their spouses—laughed.

"Okay, we're almost at the last one. Let's have one of just the family."

Jess stepped back as they took this one, and then the photographer took individual family portraits with Ellie and Jasper. Around them, the hustle and bustle of the Reilly family showed just how much it had grown in recent years. There was Dermott and Mindy and their two sons. Jackson cradled Lexi's stomach, as if imagining their own addition to the family soon. Ellie and Jasper, and Beth Reilly next to Ellie, with Mitchell on the other side.

"Now, let's include the bridesmaids in this one."

Cooper gestured for Jess to join him, and she reveled in Cooper's arms around her waist, his warmth at her back. It wasn't a cold day, but the clouds kept shifting and obscuring the sun, which meant the photographer had to work quickly in order to make the most of the sunshine while it lasted.

She glanced across to where Georgia moved next to Mitchell. Georgia had been chosen as Ellie's other bridesmaid, and it had been interesting seeing those two interact.

"Okay, we're almost there. Let's finish with a fun one, and have all the couples kissing. And yes, it doesn't have to be a kiss on the lips, a kiss on the cheek would be just as fun."

"I know what kind of kiss I want," Cooper murmured.

So did she. But part of her was also highly tempted to see

what kind of kiss Mitchell Reilly would plant on Georgia Darcy. And just what Georgia's grandmother might say if she ever saw.

But as soon as Cooper drew near, all other thoughts fled as the intensity in his eyes drew her heart fluttering. And when the photographer did the countdown, and Cooper pressed his lips to hers, she closed her eyes and leaned back in a swoon-worthy pose she thought even Grace Kelly would approve.

Cooper Reilly was worth swooning over. A man who loved God, a gentleman, and so handsome. He even liked animals. Just like her original Dream Match had said. He was hardworking, honest, humble, with a sense of humor, and appreciated the simple things in life. He was genuine, and judging from the way he kissed her now, he was hers.

"Okay, okay, I can see some of you enjoyed that a little too much. Others, well...." The photographer shot Georgia an apologetic look.

What had happened that she'd missed? Now she really wanted to know.

"Okay, I know I said that was the last one but let's just do one more while the light is good. Look this way and everyone say 'congratulations, Jasper and Ellie.'"

"Congratulations, Jasper and Ellie," Jess echoed.

"Congratulations, Jess and Cooper," Cooper murmured for her ears only.

She laughed, gazing up at him, a question in her eyes.

One he had every intention of answering before too much time passed.

"Eyes this way. Now, that's perfect." The photographer checked her camera. "Yep, that should do. Thanks, one and all."

"You're very welcome." An excuse to hold Jess in public? Yes, please, and thank you.

A gong announced that they were about to commence the meal. It was being catered by the Bellbird café, who had partnered with Joe's Diner to create a fun mix of delicate finger food and homespun diner classics to satisfy all taste buds. And with the amazing dessert creations, and the cake he couldn't wait to taste, it looked to be a great night of eating ahead.

The meal was enjoyed, the music— solid country classics— enticing various people to sway as they moved to the various food stations to get their meals. When Ellie had said she wanted to keep things simple and rustic, Cooper hadn't thought she'd meant this simple and rustic, but it worked. And whatever the cost he was willing to pay it, the cost of the reception being the responsibility of the bride's family after all.

"This is so fun," Jess said, as she took a plate of brisket to her seat.

"I love that it's so relaxed and not pretentious."

He glanced over to where his brother sat, vainly trying to get Georgia to pay attention to him again. He wasn't having much luck.

But everyone else seemed to be having a good time. He glanced at his mom, who was happily talking with Mr. Johnson. It was interesting how he'd been seated next to her, but from the comments he had heard from his siblings it seemed everyone approved.

How good it was to be able to be here and be relaxed enjoying each other's company. This was what small towns and big families were about, connecting, being real, relating. He felt blessed to be here.

Finally the time came for the bride and groom to share a waltz, and he leaned his arm across the back of Jess's chair as they watched his sister dance with her new groom. Those two would do well.

"Now it's time for the other members of the bridal party to join in."

"Want to dance?"

"Only if it's with you."

They swayed in each other's arms, which only fueled impatience for him to get her alone. So when the next song came on, something more upbeat, he took the opportunity to take her outside, where spring blossoms in white urns trailed delicately.

"It's so beautiful," Jess said, admiring the setting. "I'm not surprised though, considering all the work she's put into things."

"If she can revive a historical museum from the dead, then she can put her sparkle into a wedding."

"It's been very sparkly." She pointed to the rhinestones on her skirt. "I gotta admit I was a little surprised to see these, but it makes sense, I suppose, if the bride is a fan of a singer who sings about Rhinestone Cowboys."

He laughed. "That's probably more my mom."

"Who is here tonight with a very eligible date, huh?"

Cooper smiled. "It is nice to see her happy."

"She deserves it." She snuggled into his shoulder.

"As do you." He pressed a kiss to her forehead.

"It seems like your mom isn't the only one enjoying a spot of dancing in the moonlight." She motioned to where Cooper's brother Mitchell was talking with Georgia Darcy.

"I can't see that one working out."

"Why not?"

"Georgia Darcy is all class, and my brother?"

"Come on. He's handsome, although not as handsome as another Reilly I happen to know, but I'm sure some women find that beard attractive."

"Hmm. Are you saying you like beards?"

"No. I think cheek stubble is beardy enough." She placed a hand on his cheek. "And far sexier to look at. And far nicer to kiss."

"You sure you don't want me going all Old Man of the Sea? I would do that for you."

"Please don't."

"Okay, fine."

"Thank you."

He chuckled. "But seriously? You think Mitch and Georgia have a shot?"

"Of course they do. But just because they have a shot doesn't mean he'll take it. Or that she'll agree."

"I can't see her grandmother ever agreeing. From the things I've heard her say she's got high hopes for Georgia that go way higher than an NHL player."

"Hockey players still manage to win the hearts of ladies. Carrie Underwood married Mike Fisher, and he used to play pro hockey."

"Now that's a country star I like." He grinned at her. "Not as much as a certain brunette of course."

"Of course."

The music changed, this time shifting to a song they recognized.

"I like this song."

"Me too."

They glanced across to where Ellie had finally taken to the dance floor again with Jasper, who seemed delighted to have the chance to hold her in his arms again.

"I think Ellie is more a fan of Keith Urban, to be honest."

"That's very understandable. He has good songs."

"You mean like loving 'Somebody Like You'?"

"Uh huh."

He wrapped an arm around her. "Or being 'Tangled Up in Love'?"

"Sure."

"What about 'Only You Can Love Me'?"

"I like that one too." She studied him.

"Because you know it's true. I could never love anyone else. It's only you. It's always been you. I could never even think of anyone else."

She stroked his cheek. "I get that impression."

"Yeah? How so?"

"When you kiss me," she murmured.

"Is that an invitation?"

"Always."

He took his time kissing her, exploring her mouth with his, and she pressed closer and closer until daylight—or starlight— had no way to get in.

Finally he pulled back with a sigh. "You kiss way too good."

"You can't kiss alone."

He smiled, and pressed another kiss to her lips. "I don't want to wait a second longer for our future to begin."

"What are you saying?"

"You, Jess. I want you. I want to marry you, for us to have this," he gestured to where Dermott and Mindy played with their children, then pointed to where Jackson cradled Lexi's tiny baby bump. "I want to live in Trinity Lakes with you forever and raise kids and all kinds of animals and live happily ever after with you." He exhaled. "And I know this isn't polished or pretty or anything like the proposal you deserve, but I want to be the one who makes you smile every day, who is the sunshine in your storms, who points to Jesus as our true north, who is your knight in shining armor. I love you, Dr. Jessica Martin, and I want to love and bless you all the days of my life. Please say you'll be mine."

She studied him, her heart expanding. "Of course I'll say yes. I love you too."

They kissed, and the night filled with starlight and promise, as the Reilly barn filled with love and laughter.

Of all the men in all the world, only he could love her.

The End.

Now the only Reilly who needs to find love is Mitchell. Find out his story in *Plays By the Book*.

And don't forget to check out the next book in the Trinity Lakes series, *Like Stars that Shine* by Jenny Glazebrook.

A NOTE FROM THE AUTHOR

Thank you for reading *Only You Can Love Me*, the fifteenth book in the Trinity Lakes romance series. *Only You Can Love Me* continues to follow the lives and loves of the Reilly family first mentioned in *Love Somebody Like You* (Jackson & Lexi's story) and *Tangled Up in Love* (Ellie & Jasper's story). Several years ago I was lucky enough to visit some gorgeous towns like Walla Walla and Chelan in Washington state, and it was fun to work with other authors to create the Trinity Lakes series based on these places. If you've enjoyed this book, please check out the pictures from my visit to Washington on my website at www.carolyn-millerauthor.com

———

Reviews help other readers find new-to-them authors, so if you can spare a moment to write a quick review at Goodreads / your place of purchase, I'd be very grateful.

Huge thanks to the wonderful ladies of my ARC team for all your help and support. I appreciate you, and all my wonderful readers!

Make sure you check out Mitchell's story in *Plays by the Book*. And if you've enjoyed this taste of small town life then I hope you'll read the Muskoka Romance series, that starts with *Muskoka Shores*.

If you enjoy Christian contemporary romance you may want to check out the books in the Original Six hockey romance series, a sweet & swoony, slightly sporty Christian contemporary romance series.

The Breakup Project
Love on Ice
Checked Impressions
Hearts and Goals
Big Apple Atonement
Muskoka Blue

Romance and hockey fans may also want to read *Fire and Ice*, the first book in the Northwest Ice series, which includes a book about Mitch, the final Reilly brother, and his quest to find love in *Plays by the Book*. (And you can find out about Dermott and Mindy's love story in the Independence Islands series, starting with *Restoring Fairhaven*)

I'd love for you to check out my other books and to sign up for my newsletter at www.carolynmillerauthor.com where you can be the first to learn all my book and contest news, and discover more behind-the-book details and photos. Newsletter subscribers can also get an exclusive bonus book free, so grab your copy of *Originally Yours* by visiting www.carolynmiller author.com today.

ALSO IN THE TRINITY LAKES ROMANCE SERIES

Next in the Trinity Lakes Romance series

Book #16 - *Like Stars that Shine* by Jenny Glazebrook

She is running home. He has never had a home.

Esther Ladan has lost all confidence in her ability to read people. A very public break-up with her boyfriend has dealt a devastating blow to her heart and her pride.

Now two of the town's most big-hearted, big-mouthed elderly ladies are determined to find her perfect match.

After years in witness protection, **Tanner Elliott** is finally free to live his life without looking over his shoulder. Still, he's learned to be more observant than most and he's an expert in reading body language.

When Esther asks him to scrutinize the dates her friends arrange for her, the results are not what either of them expect.

Can Esther and Tanner overcome their difficult pasts, learn to trust Jesus with their hearts, and shine for Him in a broken world?

Welcome to Trinity Lakes, the warm and welcoming small town in east Washington state filled with charm, family, and friends, where fresh starts, second chances, and romance abounds. You'll meet cowboys and swoony bachelors, sweet and sassy ladies, and your new best friends. This series of sweet and clean standalone Christian romances will warm your heart, inspire your faith, and bring a smile to your soul.

Check out the other books in the Trinity Lakes series:

Never Find Another You - Narelle Atkins

The Ocean Between Us - Meredith Resce

I'll Always Choose You - Lisa Renee

Always By My Side - Iola Goulton

Love Somebody Like You - Carolyn Miller

Where Our Hearts Lie - Jenny Glazebrook

No Matter How Far - Sara Beth Williams

Over the Rainbow - Meredith Resce

Tangled Up in Love - Carolyn Miller

In Truth and Love - Jenny Glazebrook

Blue Skies Dreaming - Amanda Deed

Yesterday, Now and Always - Sara Beth Williams

Right in Front of You - Jessica Wakefield

Always in My Heart - Iola Goulton

Only You Can Love Me - Carolyn Miller

Like Stars that Shine - Jenny Glazebrook

My Achy Broken Heart - Meredith Resce

ABOUT THE AUTHOR

Carolyn Miller lives in the beautiful Southern Highlands of New South Wales, Australia, with her husband and four children. A long-time lover of romance, especially that of Jane Austen, Georgette Heyer and LM Montgomery, Carolyn loves to write contemporary and historical romance that draws readers into fictional worlds that show the truth of God's grace in our lives.

To find out more about Carolyn's books, and to subscribe to her newsletter, please visit www.carolynmillerauthor.com. By subscribing, you can also get a free novella, Originally Yours.

You can also connect with her at

Muskoka Holiday Morsels

Muskoka Promise

Muskoka Miracle

<u>Trinity Lakes collection</u>

Love Somebody Like You

Tangled Up in Love

Only You Can Love Me

<u>Our House on Sycamore Street</u>

The Lost Daughter's Irishman

<u>The Fairall Romance Legacy</u>

An Irish Kiss

<u>The Greener Gardens Romance series</u>

Restoring Fairhaven

Regaining Mercy

Reclaiming Hope

Rebuilding Hearts

Refining Josie

Historical:

<u>Regency Wallflowers</u>

Dusk's Darkest Shores

Midnight's Budding Morrow

Dawn's Untrodden Green

<u>Regency Brides: Legacy of Grace</u>

The Elusive Miss Ellison

The Captivating Lady Charlotte

The Dishonorable Miss DeLancey

<u>Regency Brides: Promise of Hope</u>

Winning Miss Winthrop

Miss Serena's Secret

The Making of Mrs Hale

<u>Regency Brides: Daughters of Aynsley</u>

A Hero for Miss Hatherleigh

Underestimating Miss Cecilia

Misleading Miss Verity

'Heaven and Nature Sing' from the Joy to the World Christmas
novella collection

'More than Gold' from

the Across the Shores novella collection

'Convincing the Circuit Preacher' from

The Courting the Country Preacher novella collection

www.ingramcontent.com/pod-product-compliance
Lightning Source LLC
Chambersburg PA
CBHW032000180726
48283CB00008B/2511